Scoundrel's Redemption

Highlander's Pact, Book Three

By

Sky Purington

Text by Sky Purington
Cover by Wicked Smart Designs

Dragonblade Publishing, Inc. is an imprint of Kathryn Le Veque Novels, Inc.
P.O. Box 7968
La Verne CA 91750
ceo@dragonbladepublishing.com

Produced in the United States of America

First Edition December 2020
Print Edition

The characters and events portrayed in this book are fictitious. Any similarity to real persons, living or dead, is purely coincidental and not intended by the author.

ARE YOU SIGNED UP FOR DRAGONBLADE'S BLOG?

You'll get the latest news and information on exclusive giveaways, exclusive excerpts, coming releases, sales, free books, cover reveals and more.

Check out our complete list of authors, too!

No spam, no junk. That's a promise!

Sign Up Here

www.dragonbladepublishing.com

Dearest Reader;

Thank you for your support of a small press. At Dragonblade Publishing, we strive to bring you the highest quality Historical Romance from the some of the best authors in the business. Without your support, there is no 'us', so we sincerely hope you adore these stories and find some new favorite authors along the way.

Happy Reading!

CEO, Dragonblade Publishing

Additional Dragonblade books by Author Sky Purington

Highlander's Pact Series

Scoundrel's Vengeance (Book 1)

Scoundrel's Fortune (Book 2)

Scoundrel's Redemption (Book 3)

About the Book

A widowed Englishwoman with a difficult past and a battle-weary broken Highlander come together in a tale of redemption.

Haunted by a dark past and resolved to a loveless future, Greer Hastings has accepted her lot in life. She will marry a man of her uncle's choosing to better their family's station. First, however, she will see her friend and her children freed from her uncle's clutches. An impossible feat. Or so it seems until her long-lost mother returns alongside a Scotsman who makes an offer she can't refuse.

Teagan MacLauchlin will do whatever it takes to see through the pact he made with his brothers. Marry to fill the clan's coffers. What he doesn't expect is a lass as broken as he on the other side of that bargain. Someone truly in need of saving. Determined to free Greer from her greedy uncle and depraved fiancé, he'll do anything to get her out of there. Even if means bringing the wrath of two English barons down on his head.

Embarking on a dangerous rescue mission in hostile territory, Teagan and Greer navigate the treacherous English-Scottish border on an adventure for the ages. One fraught with not just the monsters chasing them but the demons from their past.

Can two damaged hearts come together amidst so much turmoil? Or will what haunts them ultimately drive them apart?

Prologue

French Border 1343

EVERYTHING HAD GONE quiet.

Deadly silent.

Teagan crept through the woodland with a keen eye on his surroundings, bracing for an unexpected attack.

Yet none came.

All remained silent.

Eerily still.

Until an all-too-familiar sound filled the sky.

"Something's not right." Edmund's gaze rose to the vultures circling overhead. "Trouble lies ahead."

He and his comrade in-arms had just left a skirmish with the English to pursue a few cowards. After cutting them down swiftly, they were about to turn back only to sense trouble.

"Do ye hear that?" Teagan murmured.

"Aye." Edmund listened closely. "Sounds like men moving further away from us."

"Not away from us, but what lies ahead." He held his sword at the ready when cottages appeared. "'Tis a village."

Or at least it was.

He'd seen horrible things since fighting on behalf of Scotland's Auld Alliance with France, but nothing compared to what they came upon that day. Broken, bloodied bodies. Awful carnage. Unspeakable atrocities done to women.

After Teagan gestured that Edmund go in one direction and he another, Teagan made his way deeper into the village.

"Bloody *hell*," he cursed when he rounded a corner and came upon a scene no one should witness, let alone suffer.

Not bothering with stealth, he roared, "Nay," and yanked a man off a lass. Shaking with fury, he punched him once, twice, then a third time before he slit his throat.

"'Tis all right, lass," he said gently, returning to the woman's side. She struggled to breathe as he covered her with his cloak and held her hand. "All will be well."

But it would not be.

Not at all.

Her pained gaze drifted to his face, then went vacant moments later.

Just like that, she was gone.

Trembling with rage, he closed her eyes to death, hung his head, and murmured a prayer for her soul. This sort of thing happened far too often during wartime, and he'd long ago reached his breaking point. Long ago, given up hope good still existed in the world.

"Och," Edmund said softly when he joined him and saw the woman. He made the sign of the cross on his chest. "Bunch of bloody monsters."

"We should look for survivors." Teagan ground his teeth and headed deeper into the village. "Mayhap, some lived."

How could they have, though? Whoever did this had been brutal. Ruthless.

"There." Edmund pointed ahead. "I just saw a lass."

They headed that way, only to discover two women fleeing into the forest.

Moments later, a young man leapt out of nowhere with his sword at the ready, blocking their attempt to follow.

"You will g-g-go no further," he stuttered. Though shaking, he held his ground and narrowed his eyes at Teagan and Edmund. "In the n-name of Good King Edward III, you will stand d-down and leave those w-women be."

"*Good* King Edward?" Edmund sneered in disgust. "There is nothing good about him. Now get out of our way."

Assuming the man would flee in terror, Edmund made a motion like he was going to engage, only for their opponent to stay put. Though he shook so hard he could barely hold his sword up, he was brave.

"What happened here?" Teagan growled. "Who did this?"

The man was about to respond but stumbled back a few steps instead, his eyes wide with fear. Teagan realized why when he glanced over his shoulder. His men were approaching. Yet it wasn't them the man's eyes locked on. Nay, another group came from the opposite direction.

Clearly only so courageous, the man fled when the groups engaged one another.

"Let him go," Teagan said when Edmund started after him. "He obviously means to protect the lasses and our men need help."

That decision, it just so happened, would someday prove very helpful.

Chapter One

MacLauchlin Castle
Scotland 1347

THOUGH EAGER TO leave, Teagan waited patiently while everyone said their goodbyes.

"You will bring her back safely?" Julianna looked at him with her heart in her eyes. "You promise?"

"Enough with that already, daughter." Cecille shot him an apologetic look. "He, *we*, will do our very best to bring your sister, Greer, home safely."

"Aye." Teagan winked at Julianna behind her mother's back. "And ye can ask me as much as ye like."

Cecille and Julianna had traveled with Isabella when she fled France back at Hogmanay. Since then Isabella had married his brother, Malcolm and everyone had settled at MacLauchlin Castle. Now, determined to bring her daughter Greer home from England after having been separated for years, Cecille would be joining him on the journey south.

Meeting young Julianna and her mother, Cecille last winter had been a breath of fresh air in his haunted existence. Ten years of battling in France, then on behalf of Scotland's King David II, had taken its toll.

Those moments in the village, especially so.

Since then, he'd been tormented, wondering how he might have changed things. Mayhap if he'd gotten there sooner? While he knew better than to think he and Edmund alone could have downed them all, mayhap he could have gone for help. Gotten men back there before too much harm was done.

"Have ye everything ye need, brother?" His eldest sibling and laird, Keenan, eyed the men Teagan had chosen to escort him and Cecille to the border.

"Aye." He nodded thanks to Isabella, who had prepared food for their travels. "Thanks to my new sister by marriage, we have more than enough to hold us over."

"Are ye sure ye dinnae want me to come?" his brother Malcolm said, not for the first time. He frowned and shook his head. "Ye're traveling through dangerous areas."

Though they didn't say it, his brothers worried less about attackers and more about the state of Teagan's mind. Would he be able to keep his composure through what lay ahead? Or would his demons rear their ugly heads? Their concerns were valid, too. On occasion, he couldn't see past moments from the war. The rage he'd felt in the village that day. The guilt he still carried.

"Where we travel is no more dangerous than this area." Teagan gestured at Isabella and Fionna with their swollen bellies, reminding his brothers why they need not come. "'Tis best ye protect our people and the wee ones on the way."

"I completely agree." Cecille embraced Julianna one last time, then held her at shoulder's length. "I expect you to—"

"I know." Julianna managed a smile. "Be on my best behavior, and remember we are guests here."

"Even though, in truth, ye live here now," his nephew said.

The lad's grin dropped under Cecille's stern look. "And you—"

"Will continue to be a perfect gentleman around me," Julianna intercepted. Her lips curled up ever so slightly when she looked at Dougal but dropped immediately beneath her mother's narrowed eyes.

Truth told, Julianna and Dougal were on the verge of adolescence and got along quite well, so their behavior was to be expected. It mattered not that she was English and he a Scot. Their friendship had blossomed over the past few months and their flirtatious antics hinted at things to come.

"They will be fine." Isabella glanced between Dougal and Julianna with amusement before she nodded at Cecille with reassurance. "I will make sure of it."

Cecille sighed, shook her head, and got on her horse. "One can only hope."

"Travel safe," Keenan said. "Dinnae forget to send word when ye're heading back to Scotland."

"Aye." Teagan bid everyone farewell, and at long last, nearly five months from when they hatched this plan, he and Cecille set out.

While some might worry about a woman in her middle years making such a trek, Cecille had more than proven she could take care of herself. Not only that, but she was a necessary part of their venture to retrieve Greer.

That is if she actually needed saving.

She had remained behind with her father at her uncle's estate years ago when Cecille and Julianna were sent to France. Since then, her father had left with stolen family jewels hoping to start a new life with his family. He had planned to join Cecille and Julianna, then go back and exchange one of the most priceless jewels for Greer's release. After all, Greer was valuable to her uncle. More so, the prestige she could bring him with the right marriage. Sadly enough, however, her father had died before Cecille arrived in Scotland, leaving it up to her to retrieve her daughter.

"You will help me find out either way if Greer wants to leave her uncle, yes?" Cecille had asked Teagan back at Hogmanay. "You will help me get her away if 'tis her wish?"

"Aye," he'd replied without hesitation. Not only because he liked Cecille

and Julianna but because he would never say no to a lass in trouble.

"Marrying Greer would fulfill this agreement you have with your brothers," Cecille had pointed out. "With her comes a portion of my treasure. An amount that would help fill your clan's coffers very well indeed."

"I wouldnae be marrying for love," he'd warned bluntly, preferring to be honest. "For I am nae capable, nor do I want to." Respecting her too much to do otherwise, he had looked her straight in the eyes. "Is that truly what ye want for yer daughter?" And because it mattered. "To a Scot no less?"

"You know I do not care about that," she'd replied. "I have received more kindness from your clan than I ever did from anyone in France or England." A twinkle had lit her eyes. "As to your loving Greer, time with tell."

He hadn't bothered arguing but refrained from giving any false hope as they concocted their plan. One, as luck would have it, that ended up including his wartime friend, Edmund.

"I *do* wish we could have left earlier in the year," Cecille mentioned, drawing him back to the present. They made their way into the woodland with fifteen or so men. "Though, of course, I understand the need to wait for Edmund."

Unfortunately, though eager to assist them sooner, his friend had pressing business to attend first.

"Aye," he responded. "'Twill be far easier with the elements in our favor, too."

"Quite right." Cecille lowered her hood so she could enjoy the beautiful spring day.

A handsome woman with silver-dusted brown hair, she'd had her fair share of suitors over the past few months, despite being a Sassenach. Suitors to whom she was gracious, but turned away. While some might think her a snob, he knew better. She still pined after the father of her children.

"I wonder what Greer will make of seeing me again." Cecille sighed. "We have been too long out of touch."

"I dinnae think ye should worry until ye've spoken with her." He shook his head, well aware how guilty she felt. How overly concerned.

"No matter what comes of it, at least ye'll have laid eyes on her. If nothing else, 'twill put yer mind at ease if all is well."

"True," she murmured. "Even so."

It was a conversation they'd had time and time again with no real conclusion. Nor would one come until they arrived at her brother Randolph's estate. Then they would see how all fared. Not just that, but they would see where her daughter stood in regard to the man to whom she was supposedly engaged.

To his mind, that would likely be the biggest obstacle they faced.

Something he mulled over as the day wore on, wondering what he was walking into. Not just because of Cecille's nefarious reasons for being there, but because he was a Scotsman walking into enemy territory.

"Ahh, my friend turned brother!" Edmund declared in greeting that evening when they arrived in a small village a day's ride from the border. Grinning, he embraced Teagan and clapped him on the back. "'Tis always good to see ye."

Edmund's dark hair brushed the nape of his neck, and his beard was well-trimmed. Where he'd been wiry and gaunt during the war, he now looked healthy.

Not to mention Scottish.

At least at the moment.

Teagan shook his head at Edmund when they joined him in the tavern for a dram of whisky. "Ye're verra good at what ye do, friend."

That being his ability to blend in.

Born to an English noble and a poor Scottish mother, Edmund, after years of being angry at his father during the war, had finally embraced both worlds. Which meant he could play the part of a Scotsman every bit as well as he could an Englishman. A boon when traveling between the two countries during troubling times.

"I do my best." Edmund slid a sly look Teagan and Cecille's way, his hushed tone that of a co-conspirator. "'Tis hard to believe 'tis time to put our plan into motion, aye?"

"Here's to that." Cecille held her mug up in a toast. "At long last."

They returned her toast and went over the details of their arrangement. The plan they set in motion months ago when he and Cecille were trying to figure out the best way to get Greer out of England. Ironically enough, as they had discussed it, namely Cecille's life in England before she went to France, Teagan realized there might just be a way. It turned out Edmund was the son of a baron affiliated with Cecille's kin.

That meant he was in a position to vouch for Teagan.

"I wouldnae expect a warm reception upon arrival at Randolph's holding, though," Edmund had warned when they presented the idea to him. He'd grinned all the while, enjoying a chance at a wee bit o' stealth. "But ye will be welcome enough as my half-brother." He perked a brow, reminding Teagan how things had to go. "'Twill help that ye look the part of an English sympathizer."

"Aye, I know," Teagan grumbled, hardly imagining it. "No braids and my hair pulled back."

"And no clan colors," Cecille reminded, looking him over.

"Never that," Teagan said dutifully.

Though it was hard to imagine dressing like a Sassenach, never mind pretending he sympathized with their cause, he could admit to a smidge of excitement. While glad to be home from war, outside of the occasional skirmishes, things had been quiet lately. He appreciated the hard work that came with running a castle, but he would always be a warrior at heart.

"Ye brought the jewels for bargaining, aye?" Edmund asked Cecille.

She nodded. "Yes."

"And mayhap, as I suggested when visiting a few months ago, a bible from Fulbert?" Edmund inquired. "As ye know, Greer is more pious than usual lately and spends time with God, often. I think 'twill make a good gift upon arrival."

"Yes, I have it."

"Good then." Edmund raised his mug in another toast. "Here's to a plan well executed!"

They raised their mugs as well, hoping for the best.

The best, however, as they discovered days later, upon arrival at Cecille's family home, would prove to be a struggle from the onset.

Chapter Two

Northern England

GREER MADE THE symbol of the cross over her chest and lowered her head in prayer when Bartholomew paused at the door of the chapel. She prayed that he would keep going. That he would not linger and make her uncomfortable as he so often did.

Unfortunately, he *did* linger. Even worse, he paced and cleared his throat every so often in impatience.

Biting back a sigh, she finally joined him, doing her best to muster a tepid smile.

"Did you not pray already today?" he muttered in greeting, holding out the crook of his elbow. "Walk with me, Greer."

Not a question but an order.

While tempted to tell him she had no desire to walk with him, let alone touch him, she knew better, so took his arm and headed down the corridor. She had spent enough years under the thumb of her domineering, cruel uncle to recognize the same traits in Bartholomew. Traits that he had already exhibited several times over the past few months. So she knew it best to be compliant lest risk his considerable temper.

Older than her by nearly two decades, wrinkles fanned out from the corners of Bartholomew's eyes. She often wondered about that because he rarely, if ever, smiled. He was, however, quite good at grimacing. With an overly long forehead and too-thin face, he had likely never been a handsome man. But he'd always been a well-titled one from a prominent family.

That, regrettably, gave him the choice of any bride he wished.

She, of course, had no say in the matter.

Sometimes she pondered what it would be like if she were in charge. If *she* ruled this estate and told her uncle what he could and could not do. She might have responded to Bartholomew far differently if that were the case.

When Bartholomew announced with a haughty, she-should-be-grateful look that he would take her as his wife, she would have told him quite politely that he would not. That if, and only if, she entertained the idea, he would go about things correctly. Because how one appeared meant little to her.

How they acted, on the other hand, meant a great deal.

"Oh, but you are a dreamer!" her dear friend Margery would have said.

"Am I?" she'd reply in turn. "Is it too much to ask that he might woo me? Respect me?" She would shake her head. "I'm not looking for love, I hardly believe in it, but some respect would be nice."

Unfortunately, Margery had died years ago. Since then, she had become a comforting voice in Greer's mind, helping her get through life. Helping her cope not only with something traumatic that had happened in her past but with the horrible men she'd dealt with since her family left. Not just her uncle and Bartholomew, but the old man she'd been married off to. Her late husband had been just as overbearing if not more so.

"Are you listening to me, Greer?" Bartholomew asked, interrupting her thoughts.

"Of course," she lied, biting back another sigh. Quite frankly, she preferred the calm of her own thoughts to conversing with most people nowadays.

"Good, then you agree pushing our wedding up is for the best." The lust in his gaze when he looked at her chest rather than her face matched his crude words. "For as you know, I wish to sire a son.

Sooner rather than later."

"Then look me in the eyes, you miscreant," she envisioned saying. "And at least pretend you care what I think rather than how I look!"

Needless to say, she said no such thing.

"Of course," she said again dutifully, lowering her head to please him. When did he want to push their betrothal up to? Panic simmered beneath the surface, but she kept it well hidden. "Whatever you think is best, my lord."

"Good." The red that had bubbled up in his face drained. "Less than a month from today, then."

Less than a month? From today? To Bartholomew? Dear God, no.

He was about to say something else when a commotion outside caught their attention.

"Who is that?" He frowned out the window at three people approaching on horseback. "They seem to be creating quite a stir."

By stir, he meant her uncle's men coming to attention on the curtain wall and in the courtyard. She tried to see those approaching more clearly, but they were too far off.

"Stay here," Bartholomew ordered. "I will go see to this."

See to this as though he owned the castle, not her uncle.

She wrung her hands, mulling over what to do next.

"You know what you need to do," Margery would have said.

She nodded. "Right, yes, stay." Then she shook her head. "Or mayhap 'twould be better if I made sure all was well belowstairs."

Margery would agree. "It really would be prudent, all things considered."

All things being innocent children who could end up underfoot. More so, beneath her uncle's wrath. That in mind, she flew down the back way, sticking to the shadows whilst watching for the little ones who, at the moment, were nowhere to be found.

In the short time it took her to get to the courtyard, her uncle's men had intercepted the newcomers and were leading them over the drawbridge. So said the clamor of hooves on wood. Dust rained down from those getting into position on the wall walk, their arrows cocked and ready at the first sign of trouble.

"Ho there," Bartholomew called out when they were just beyond the portcullis. While that should have earned him a disgruntled look from her uncle, he'd never risk upsetting the titled baron.

"He should, though," she muttered under her breath, envisioning another response altogether.

"You have no right to greet guests in my castle," her uncle should exclaim, huffing and puffing as he was wont to do, at last seeing the light of what kind of man Bartholomew really was. "What was I ever thinking, allowing you to marry my lovely niece? She is far too good for you!"

But alas, he said no such thing, nor would he ever.

"Ho there," one of the three called back as they finally entered the courtyard, and she could see them.

She recognized the first as a distant relation to the family who visited rarely but had a prominent enough name that he was always welcome. Edmund, she believed. Handsome with dark, wavy hair and intense features, she'd always thought him rather mysterious. As though he acted one way but was someone else entirely. A spy, perhaps.

Going off her delicate frame, the second person was a woman, but she was hooded and turned away, so impossible to see.

The third figure, however, was impossible to ignore.

Had she ever seen a more striking man? With broad shoulders, thick dark blonde hair, and chiseled masculine features, she imagined he turned many a female head. *All*, for that matter. Even more noteworthy, however, at least to the storyteller in her, was his deceptively relaxed yet astute gaze. He might seem nonchalant, but she saw the way he took in the castle's curtain walls, noting the location of her uncle's men.

"Oh, but you are seeing another story unravel, are you not?" Margery would say.

"No," she would deny, already envisioning Edmund as the secret infiltrator, here to distract her uncle and Bartholomew, whilst the warrior saved her

from this awful place.

He would plunk her on his horse—plunk?—no, no, that wasn't right. It sounded quite abrupt and perhaps a bit painful. No, he would gallantly swing her up onto his horse, and they would ride off together. She would be free at last. Gone from this place of foul deeds and wrongdoings.

Yet, no such thing happened, nor would it.

She wished she could hear what was being said, but they were too far off.

"Who are they?" came a whisper from her left. Her friend's son, Duncan, had snuck out of the shadows and joined her. "I dinnae recognize them."

"Shh." She crouched and put a finger to his lips. "Lest you draw attention to yourself." When his eyes rounded in alarm, she smiled in reassurance. "Everything will be just fine. They are not here for you and your sister."

Or so she hoped.

The truth was, she had no idea.

She glanced back at the three travelers only to find the handsome warrior's gaze locked on her. A strange but pleasurable warmth swept through her when their eyes met. As if they were connected in some indefinable way.

"But of course you are," Margery would remind. "He just plunked, I mean 'swung' you onto his horse and rode off into the sunset with you."

"He's looking at ye," Duncan whispered. "My countryman sees yer magic, aye?"

Countryman? He was Scottish? How did Duncan know that?

"Can you not see it?" Margery would say. "The wild hovering just beneath the surface?"

Where a chill might have swept through some, she felt another rush of warmth. Then again, she didn't harbor the resentment her countrymen did toward the Scots. Rather, she commiserated with their misery. The feeling of forever being oppressed by someone who wanted to control and own you.

"Niece," her uncle barked, jolting her to her feet.

When Uncle Randolph scowled at Duncan, she tucked him behind her skirts and nodded.

"Well, come here already, girl!" Randolph made an exasperated come-hither motion. His thin lips slanted down, and his sparsely lashed bug-eyes rounded all the more. "You have a visitor."

"I'm not a girl anymore," she envisioned calling back. "I'm a full-grown woman, you buffoon!"

"I am nae afraid of him," Duncan said, even though his voice shook.

She wasn't surprised he'd rallied his courage so quickly. He had been working on that. When he tried to step around her, she stopped him because, truthfully, he should be afraid. Very much so when it came to her uncle.

"Go." She gestured to her uncle that she would be right there, then turned to Duncan, trying her best not to sound panicked. "You must go *now*. Right now, you hear?"

When his dirty little chin jutted out in defiance, she got as stern as she was willing to get. "Please. Now. For me."

He narrowed his eyes and scowled before he finally sighed and relented. "Aye, then."

He left as silently as he had come, used to sticking to the shadows and going unnoticed.

"Niece!" her uncle barked again, this time louder.

"Enough, Randolph," the woman exclaimed. "Her name is Greer."

She froze at the sound of the voice. One she hadn't heard in far too long. Thought she never would again. Yet when the woman pulled off her hood and looked her way, the truth was clear as day.

"'Tis your dear mother," Margery would have exclaimed, a smile in her voice. "She has arisen from the dead! How absolutely wonderful!"

No, not wonderful.

Impossible.

She shook her head, not sure she saw correctly. "It cannot be."

Should not be.

For that meant but one thing.

What some had long whispered about Greer was actually true.

Chapter Three

TEAGAN KNEW THE moment his gaze connected with the lass across the way that his life would never be the same. How could it be when he'd never felt the urge to protect another so strongly? So fiercely? And for no other reason than what he saw in her thickly lashed light blue eyes, past the kindness to the stark fear hidden beneath.

At some point, she'd witnessed sheer terror.

He had seen enough warriors post-battle to recognize it.

Felt it for so long himself that it was second nature.

It took everything to keep his hand off his weapon when her uncle barked at her to join them. Moreover, when the Englishman beside him looked at her with unabashed ownership. A look that clearly prompted Greer to finally head their way, even though she'd wanted to stay and protect the lad.

Truth told, he'd never seen a more bonnie lass. With flawless ivory skin and silky raven-colored hair peeking out beneath her wimple, she had delicate features, a full, heart-shaped mouth, and a vulnerable gentleness he'd never encountered before. A merciful spirit he feared, vipers like her uncle and the man standing beside him were quick to take advantage of.

"Greer." Emotion thickened Cecille's voice as she swung down and looked at her daughter. "'Tis so very good to see you, darling."

Greer took a few more steps, then stopped obediently when the second man gave her a stern look. She blinked several times at Cecille, as if doubting her sight, then clasped her hands in front of her and nodded hello politely.

Meanwhile, Cecille's brow furrowed. Her shoulders and features tightened.

"Surely you knew," Cecille whispered hoarsely. She cleared her throat and tried again. "Surely, you knew I would come back, daughter. That I was not gone to you forever."

Greer merely nodded graciously again, her gaze still not quite right. But then, if he wasn't mistaken, seeing her mother again shocked her. Every bit as much as a man witnessing his first death during warfare. Or, better yet, how he might respond if the dead rose from the grave.

"She thought ye dead," Teagan murmured before he could stop himself.

"Dead?" Cecille's tortured gaze stayed on Greer. She shook her head and held her arms out. "No, no, darling, I'm not dead but very much alive."

When Greer didn't respond or move but waited for permission from the men, Cecille muttered something under her breath about bloody blackguards and rushed to her daughter. Though Greer remained unresponsive when Cecille wrapped her arms around her, Teagan didn't miss the flash of emotion in her gaze.

He had expected all sorts of scenarios when he came on this venture but not this. Not a lass truly in need of saving. Not to this extent. But she did need saving, and it was never so obvious. Regrettably, it was also clear, though domineering and small-minded, how powerful her gatekeepers were.

He'd noted the number of seasoned warriors her uncle had. Too many for him and Edmund to fight alone. Even with the men they'd left at his friend's holding awaiting further word.

"Why did you think me dead?" Cecille asked Greer, tears in her eyes when she pulled back. "Who told you that?"

"I never said," Greer whispered, struggling to find her voice. Her nervous gaze flickered from Teagan to the other men, then back to her mother. She cleared her throat. "I never said I thought that."

Cecille eyed her daughter for a moment, seeing the truth of things as only a mother could. "But Teagan was right. You did." Her sharp gaze flew to her brother. "Why did she think that, Randolph? Why did my daughter think I was dead?"

"Because I assumed you *were*, sister." Randolph shrugged an overly padded shoulder. "Last I knew, you boarded a ship to Scotland and vanished. 'Twas safe to say at that point you had perished." He notched his pointy chin. "Therefore, I saw no reason to pamper the girl with falsities."

"She's not a girl but a woman," Cecille cut back.

"All the more reason to be blunt."

"You mean assume," she countered, "then flat-out lie."

"Why are you here?" Randolph snapped, exasperated. "And have you been in contact with your scoundrel of a husband at any point? For, I'm sure he stole a substantial amount from our family before he ran off and abandoned poor Greer."

Poor Greer. As if the swine cared about her in the least.

Where most probably wouldn't see it beneath Greer's reserved nature, Teagan didn't miss the flash of anguish in her eyes at the mention of her father.

"I'm here to see my beloved daughter, whom I have not seen in years, Randolph." Cecille's worried gaze lingered on Greer. "Here to make sure all is well, not cater to your paranoia about my husband."

"Rest assured, all is well with my Greer," the second man said tightly, peering down his thin, sharp blade of a nose. "We are to be married, and she is *quite* content." He nodded once as if granting her a great boon. "Eager even."

Content? Eager?

Teagan saw neither of those things beneath Greer's carefully crafted façade.

"You are to be married?" Cecille asked her daughter, feigning ignorance even as she searched for happiness on Greer's face. For any sign this was a welcome arrangement.

"Yes," Greer said softly. Her hesitant gaze flickered from her fiancé to her mother as though she wanted to say one thing but would dutifully say another. "Lord Montgomery has been very gracious, agreeing to the arrangement."

Gracious? As if he were the one who'd succumbed to marrying her. Teagan imagined it was the very opposite. If anything, the brute was desperate to get betwixt her thighs.

"I look forward to hearing more about it," Cecille managed. Her wary gaze flickered over Greer's fiancé before she made introductions.

In turn, Randolph did the same.

"I did not know you had a brother," Randolph said to Edmund. He took in Teagan, his expression bland but cordial enough. "From your Scottish side, you say?"

"Yes." Edmund gave Randolph a knowing look as he and Teagan swung off their horses. "I think you will find his take on the state of things to your liking."

"'Tis good to hear." Believing they were brothers, Randolph nodded at Teagan absently before he continued to address Edmund. "However did you and my sister cross paths?"

Teagan tuned out Edmund's well-rehearsed explanation about hearing rumor of her whereabouts and watched Greer discreetly. Though her narrow shoulders were tight, as if she'd give anything to dash away, she remained still with her hands clasped together and her gaze on the ground. As if she were trained to remain quiet and obsolete when men discussed important matters a lass couldn't possibly understand.

Though tempted to speak and include her in the conversation, the timing wasn't right. If anything, he would get them both in trouble.

"I thought mayhap my brother and I would stay here with Cecille for a while," Edmund went on as a stableman took their horses. He clasped Randolph on the shoulder like he was a good friend. A comrade-in-arms. "It has been a while since we enjoyed one another's company, and we are kin, albeit distant, are we not?"

"Yes, but of course." Randolph stood up a little straighter, acknowledging such. Self-importance dripped off every word. "Stay on as long as you like. Enjoy all we Hastings have to offer." His brows swept up. "Mayhap you would even like to join the festivities next month, for we have a wedding on the horizon."

Cecille visibly tensed again. Her gaze never left her daughter. "Yours then, darling?"

"Yes, *ours*," Bartholomew replied. "You are welcome to attend."

"I would think so." Cecille shot him a look. "I *am* her mother, after all." She cocked her head at Greer. "Might we spend some time together? Catch up?"

"Perhaps later if—"

"I do believe I'm addressing my daughter, not you, sir." Cecille frowned at Bartholomew and held out her elbow to Greer. "Come, let us go spend some time together. I have missed you dearly."

When Greer looked at her uncle, unsure, Randolph waved her away, obviously wanting the headache of his sister's sharp tongue silenced. "Yes, go if you must." His gaze narrowed on Cecille. "Then you and I shall talk, sister. For, I still want answers about your husband and what I'm convinced he stole from me."

Teagan wasn't surprised she made no mention of her husband's death. Not until she had a chance to tell Greer first.

Cecille nodded graciously enough at Randolph before she and Greer walked off.

Once they were gone, Teagan followed the men into Cecille's family home, not surprised when Randolph and Bartholomew ignored him. He might look the part, but his accent reminded them of where he came from. Therefore, he would always remain less-than in their eyes.

Which suited him just fine.

The less attention he received in these parts, the better.

Despite Randolph's grumblings about Cecille's husband stealing from him, Teagan wondered upon entering the sizeable great hall if her plan would work. *Would* her brother forfeit the prestige Greer's marriage could bring for an old heirloom? A mere jewel? Because he by no means lacked in wealth. Instead of rushes, woven carpets blanketed the floor, and thick tapestries adorned the wall, a good barrier against drafts. Furnishings were plentiful, and servants numerous.

So, it was safe to say, though Randolph seemed angry about his jewels being stolen, his desire for prestige could very well be greater. The sort of status Bartholomew Montgomery would bring his kin. Certainly not a poor Scot with little to his name but the horse he rode in on.

Nevertheless, Cecille was a force to be reckoned with, so he could only hope she succeeded. First, though, she needed to see where Greer really stood. What she wanted to do. Which he imagined might not be the easiest thing for her to glean considering her daughter's current state.

While the Englishmen caught up, Teagan sipped his ale and thought about Greer. What had she been through since Cecille and Julianna left years ago? What had put that look in her eyes? Might she tell him if they spent time alone? If he shared his own experiences? Or would such offend her? Somehow, he didn't think so. Based on what he'd seen of her outside with the lad, she was a protector by nature, with a sympathetic heart.

He continued mulling things over, surprised where his thoughts led him. The lengths to which he would go to pull Greer out of her shell. To steer her away from the demons that haunted her. For, he'd never shared his own. The things he saw. The guilt he carried. That he wanted to share them with Greer, having known her mere minutes was notable. Could there actually be a future for them? Not one of love because he didn't believe in it, but mayhap friendship and respect?

He would have thought yes, it *was* possible, had someone unexpected not joined them soon thereafter.

Someone who had the power to stop their scheme dead in its tracks.

Chapter Four

GREER HAD FELT many things since her mother and little sister left years ago, but nothing quite like what she felt at the moment. Her mother was here. So she wasn't seeing things. With that relief came an arrayof emotions that made focusing difficult.

Joy, frustration, and anger filled her.

Her mother remained silent until they were alone in the gardens. Once there, she pulled Greer into her arms again and held on tight. Still stunned and not sure how to respond, Greer embraced her weakly before pulling away.

"You are upset with me," her mother surmised. They continued strolling.

Though she didn't think it possible, she finally found her voice.

"Why didn't you come back or, at the very least, write to me?" Though she'd intended to sound detached, Greer sounded more sad than anything. "Why did you flee with Isabella De le Croix when you should have come home? Back to me?" She looked around as if by some miracle, her sister would appear out of thin air. "And where is dear Julianna?" She swallowed hard, envisioning the worst. "Is she all right?"

"I'm so sorry I could not write to you once I arrived in Scotland." Mother shook her head. "We couldn't risk your uncle knowing our whereabouts. He might have come for Julianna." Her pained gaze lingered on Greer's face. "All is well. Your sister is safe in Scotland with

Isabella. We are all…safe."

Scotland? Truly? Yet, that wasn't what concerned her the most.

"What is it?" She frowned. "Why do you sound so hesitant?"

"Come." Her mother sat on a bench and patted the space beside her. "Sit a moment so that I might tell you something."

She went to do as asked but hesitated, suddenly feeling defiant. This wasn't a man telling her what to do but her mother.

When would it end?

As if she recognized the mistake in her actions, her mother rephrased her wording. "Might you join me, daughter?" she asked. "I have news that you will want to hear…difficult news."

Unsure she wanted to hear it but grateful to be asked rather than ordered, she sat and folded her hands on her lap. "What is this news?"

"'Tis about your father." Cecille rested her hand over Greer's. "I'm afraid I heard news about him in Scotland…"

When she trailed off, Greer released a shaky sigh. "I had hoped it was not true." He had left without saying goodbye. Simply rode off, never to return. The last of all that was good in her world. "I had hoped the missive was wrong."

"Missive?" Mother frowned. "What missive?"

"The one sent to Uncle Randolph." She wondered at her mother's confusion. "A friend of father's wrote saying he had lost his life in an attack."

"An attack?" Her mother's finely arched brows pulled together. "That cannot be right, for that's not how it went at all." She shook her head. "What friend of father's said such? Did they give their name?"

"A grand mystery," Margery would have said. "Something is not adding up."

Greer shook her head, more curious by the moment. "No, they gave no name. Why do you ask? More so, why do you seem so surprised?"

When her mother shook her head and said nothing, Greer sighed. She was never told anything of importance. Her mind being that of a simple woman, she wasn't worth the words. More than that, many around here thought she lacked the necessary intelligence to converse. All but the Scottish children and their mother, that is. They found her quite clever and interesting.

"My brother has changed you, hasn't he?" Mother said softly. She eyed Greer with concern, seeing what most could not. But then, once upon a time, her mother had known her quite well.

"As has that man set to marry you," her mother continued. "My apologies, Greer, I hesitated to speak about your father because I feared spreading rumors or even getting your hopes up. But I see you are indeed a grown woman now with your own mind." She inhaled. "Not all that long ago, I learned of your father's passing in a Scottish seaside village. According to the kind old woman I met, he did not die in an attack, but of an illness he caught when tending to her sick husband."

"That sounds like something father would do," she conceded, missing him terribly. "Or at least the father I once knew."

The corners of her mother's mouth curled down. "You say that as though he changed?"

"He changed enough that he left without any explanation." She bit back emotions. "I lived but a few estates over, so why not say goodbye?" Greer stood, needing some space between her mother and herself. "I do not know what to tell you about his death other than what I already divulged."

"What do you mean you lived a few estates over?" Her mother's brows snapped together, and she stood as well. "Why were you not living here?"

"Why do you think?" she envisioned replying hotly, trying to keep bad memories of the baron she was married to before at bay. *"What would you imagine your brother would do with me in your absence? In your assumed death?"*

"It no longer matters," she said softly instead. While tempted to storm away, she was raised with better manners than that. "Father left without saying goodbye, plain and simple."

"It *does* matter," her mother insisted. "Why were you not..."

She trailed off, stunned, evidently figuring it out.

"He did *not*," her mother ground out. "Tell me my brother has not already married you off once? Not after what you had been through?"

"He knows nothing of that," she whispered, mortified her mother brought it up. That she would dare mention old demons. Events that no longer mattered.

Her past was in the past.

"Is it, though?" Margery would say. "Because I'm not so sure of that."

"Of course it is," she muttered under her breath, then cursed when she realized she'd said the words aloud.

Though renewed concern flashed in her mother's eyes, she made no mention of Greer's comment.

Having had more than enough of this, she needed time alone. To go someplace quiet and reflect. Too many underused emotions were bubbling to the surface.

"I must go." She curtsied, praying her mother gave no issue. "I have..." *What did she have? What was she saying?* "Something pressing to see to."

"More pressing than reuniting with your long-lost mother?" Margery echoed.

Worry only pushed her mother's brows together more, but thankfully, she nodded. "Of course, dear. We will talk again soon?"

"Yes." She curtsied once more and did her best to walk rather than run out of there.

The moment she was around the corner and out of sight, she leaned back against the wall and breathed a sigh of relief. Why couldn't she be stronger? Why couldn't she just say how she felt to her mother?

"You have no right to show up out of nowhere and bring up my past when you abandoned me," she should have voiced with heated passion and self-confidence. Not too much heat, though. There was something to

be said for calm intensity. That in mind, she should have narrowed her eyes and spoken with authority because *she* was in control of herself, nobody else. Or so she liked to imagine despite it being the furthest thing from the truth.

A tug on her skirt brought her out of her daydream.

"Hello, there." She smiled down at Duncan's sister, Besse, with her golden locks.

"Hello." Besse's big green eyes were round as saucers. "Did ye see them? The new characters?"

She referred to Greer's mother and those with whom she traveled.

"I did." Greer crouched, glancing left and right as if they shared a secret and spies might be listening. She leaned close and whispered, "What do you make of them?"

"I dinnae know." Besse slid a sly little look toward the back stairs. "But mayhap ye can tell me, aye? Mayhap spin yer magic?"

She smirked. "Are you asking me to spy on our visitors?"

Besse nodded, knowing Greer would never tell.

Enjoying being with Besse and Duncan almost as much as spending time alone, Greer pretended to think about it before she nodded. "All right, but you must be very, very quiet. Can you do that?"

The girl's eyes lit up, and she nodded with excitement.

"Okay, then." Greer took her hand, and they headed up until they were in one of several hallways overlooking the great hall. Crouching behind a pillared balustrade cast in shadows, they peeked through with no risk of detection. Nor, with all the bustling castle activity below, could they be heard.

Disappointment flashed in Besse's eyes. She pouted at the men sitting in front of the fire. "Och, he isnae down there anymore."

"Who?" But Greer knew. Edmund's brother. The Scotsman called Teagan. Her dashing ride-off-into-the-sunset hero.

"The big warrior with the sad eyes."

He *did* have sad eyes, didn't he? Soulful, thickly-lashed, deep brown eyes that looked as haunted as she felt. How she'd wanted to stare at him when she joined everyone earlier but didn't dare. Bartholomew was always watching and quick to jealousy. She could only imagine how he would have responded had she dared cast a glance at a younger man.

Especially one who was not only Scottish but put him to shame physically.

"Well, of course, our warrior-hero is not there right now," she whispered, spinning her 'magic' as Besse and Duncan liked to call it. "For he is doing a sweep of the castle to see what his men are up against before they raid the estate and steal us away."

"I thought that might be it." Besse's eyes rounded again. "Where will they take us?"

"To his castle, naturally. A place where you do not have to hide in corners anymore. Where you can speak your mind, within the realm of good manners that is, and smile and laugh in the open."

Where some might say it cruel to give children like Besse and Duncan false hope, she knew better than anyone how important hope really was. It allowed one to get out of bed in the morn. To get through their day, then start all over the next. For poor Scottish children like Besse and her brother with nothing but a bleak future ahead, she saw no harm in it.

But then, one way or another, she was determined to get them out of here before her uncle sold them off. Because he would. He had before. It mattered naught that their mother was here because she would be sold as well. Or kept and used for free labor and other unsavory purposes.

"I have never seen a place like that." Besse shook her head. "Do ye think his sweep is going well? That he will save us soon?"

While she knew it wrong to put such responsibility on a perfect stranger, she truly did mean to see it through herself somehow. Now that her mother was here, perhaps there might be a way. If Cecille would agree to such. For it would mean a great deal of stealth lest she risk Randolph's considerable wrath.

"I think 'tis verra likely yer warrior-hero will save ye," came another whisper. "And save ye soon."

It took her a moment to realize that hadn't been a voice in her head.

Rather, it had been the voice of the last person she expected.

Chapter Five

Teagan was never so relieved when a servant offered to show him to his chambers. He knew it was so Randolph and Bartholomew could speak privately with Edmund about him, and that was fine. He had faith in his friend to play the part well.

They had been lucky when a man named Alfred made no comment upon joining them. Unbelievably enough, he was the very soldier Teagan and Edmund had come upon in that border village during the war. The one who had defended the lasses. It seemed he was a cousin of the family and resided at the castle but most likely because of his stutter, was not welcome during a "gentleman's" conversation. Or so Teagan assumed when he was dismissed almost as soon as he arrived.

Over the course of an ale, Randolph and Bartholomew had spent more time looking at Teagan haughtily than anything else. Not to be mistaken with the flashes of disgust in their eyes. It mattered little that he was an English sympathizer, for, at the end of the day, he would still be Scottish. He would still be their long-time nemesis.

To be expected, they asked pertinent questions. Ones he answered readily enough, sure to look mightily impressed by the castle, not to mention the men themselves. That they would honor him with an audience. What more could a simple Scot ask for? 'Twas a bloody dream come true.

Or so they thought.

The moment he was shown his quarters, rather surprised he wasn't given a stall in the stables instead, he set out to explore, grateful for some time alone. Or, if he were to be honest, hopeful that he would run into Greer. That he might finally introduce himself properly and exchange a word or two with her.

An opportunity, it just so happened, that presented itself shortly after that in a hallway near the top of the castle. As good at stealth as his brother, Malcolm, he kept to the shadows, then crouched near Greer and a little girl, talking in hushed tones. Also very good at hearing, he caught every word exchanged. Despite his realistic view of the world, he found their conversation endearing.

He couldn't help but participate when the opportunity arose.

"I think 'tis verra likely yer warrior-hero will save ye," he whispered loud enough for them to hear when the little girl asked if Teagan—hero that they painted him—might save them.

He would, too. By all that was holy, he meant it. He need not know them to feel this way, either. Just off what he'd seen of this place so far, he would bring the whole of the MacLauchlin Clan down on Randolph and his self-important sidekick Bartholomew if given half the chance.

"Go on now," Greer whispered to the wee lassie before he had a chance to say it was unnecessary. She need not flee. It seemed, however, much like the lad who had stubbornly tried to stay with her earlier, the little girl wasn't going anywhere.

Rather, much to Greer's obvious mortification based on her widening eyes, she headed Teagan's way.

"Hello," the girl whispered. She looked around for intruders before daring to speak to him in their native language. *"An tàinig thu dha-rìribh gus ar sàbhaladh an uairsin?"*

"Aye, I'm truly here to save ye if ye're in need of saving, lassie." He asked her if her parents were here as well. *"A bheil do phàrantan an seo cuideachd?"*

Just her mother and brother, she replied.

"My apologies," Greer said, joining them. "She...we..." She cleared her throat, blushing prettily. "We were just enjoying the view from up here. It really is a nice hall..."

The way she trailed off and her cheeks flamed crimson gave away how embarrassed she truly was.

"*'Tis* a nice view." Determined to put her at ease, he smiled and gestured that they join him. "Though 'tis a bit smoky from the fire up here, aye? Mayhap some fresh air would be good? Mayhap even a tour of the grounds?" He knew that probably wasn't proper to ask, given they'd only just met, but he could care less. Unless it got her in trouble. "If ye think 'tis appropriate, that is?"

"Oh, *'tis*," the little girl exclaimed, introducing herself as Besse.

"Nice to meet ye, Besse. I'm Teagan." He winked at her. "Or yer warrior-hero. Whichever ye prefer." He perked a brow at Greer. "My full name is Teagan MacLauchlin, though. 'Tis a pleasure to meet ye, lass."

Her gaze found his face before it dropped obediently. "And you."

"Why are ye lookin' at the floor, mistress—" Besse began before he gently cut her off.

"Likely because she has the magic to see right through it to the level below," he admonished, gesturing that Besse lead the way, "then straight out to where the air is fresh and the springtime bountiful."

"She *does* have magic," Besse conceded. As they headed downstairs, the wee lass shared more than he imagined Greer was comfortable with. "'Tis the magic o' stories like ye couldnae imagine."

"Aye, then?" He smiled at Greer over his shoulder, only for her to avert her eyes and blush even more if such was possible. "I do love a good story."

"Well, then, ye should spend plenty o' time with Mistress Greer if—"

Besse stopped mid-sentence when her brother called out, and they were only halfway down the stairs that her mother was looking for her. She sighed and went to race off but paused when Greer cleared her throat. In turn, Besse faced them again and curtsied. "'Twas nice to meet ye, warrior-hero Teagan."

Before he could respond, she was gone, and he and Greer were alone.

"Might we continue on?" he asked, praying she would agree. "'Tis a bonnie estate and a lovely day for a stroll."

She swallowed hard, clearly wanting to say one thing but voicing another. "I should not."

"Have ye a commitment then?" he asked, even though he knew full well what she referred to. Bartholomew would not like it. "For, I could use the company."

That was no lie, either. Or should he say when it came to her, he desperately wanted it? Not because she was utterly lovely, and he was essentially here to woo her, but because he sensed she needed company as much as he. A perfect stranger to talk to that might understand where she came from. A fellow haunted soul.

Greer shook her head, crushing all hope before she surprised him and replied the opposite. "Well, perhaps just a quick stroll." She pointed ahead. "Go right at the bottom of the stairs. There is a nice stretch of woodland that affords...peace."

He knew she meant to say "privacy" for fear of her overbearing fiancé seeing them. In all actuality, he preferred that description. For it felt peaceful being around her.

"This way." Greer grabbed a basket once they were outside and headed down a path into the thick woodland beyond the castle's outer wall. "If you think the estate's beautiful, then you should see the area just around the bend."

She picked up her pace a little, almost as if she were running from something. Not surprising, considering what she dealt with here. While yes, some of her rushing might have to do with someone seeing them, he suspected it was also a need for escape.

Though a gentleman would insist they stay within sight of others, or at least get a chaperone, he couldn't seem to bring himself to do it. Mostly because he understood how she felt, he'd felt something similar when Keenan and Malcolm went off with Fionna last autumn, and he was left behind. Then the same sensation when he'd initially thought Malcolm wouldn't let him join him on his venture north to retrieve Isabella.

Whilst Greer's reasons were no doubt more extreme, he suspected her need to break free was similar to his own. Not just free of her physical barriers but those in her mind. Those that kept her trapped in another time and place.

"Yes, I know," she whispered.

"What was that?" he asked, assuming she'd been talking to him.

She shook her head and came up with an explanation he sensed had nothing to do with what she'd said.

"I said, I know," she replied. "I know 'tis just ahead."

"Aye, then." He kept a cordial smile for the first time in longer than he could remember. Not only because he wanted her to feel at ease but because, quite honestly, being with her felt natural.

She slowed, then stopped beside a tree overlooking a river. Lined with silver birches and towering beech trees with thick twisted trunks, he understood her draw to the location. Rather than sit on the bench provided, she gazed out over the water, her eyes adrift for a moment.

"'Tis a bonnie spot." He got the sense it meant a great deal to her. "'Tis special to ye, aye?"

"Yes," she whispered before she cleared her throat and gestured back the way they had come. "I suppose that must seem strange to you given the wealth of my surroundings and the beauty of my uncle's castle."

"Nay." He admired the water curling around moss-covered rocks and the trees swaying in the wind. "I think this is worth far more than the castle. I ken why ye enjoy it here." He glanced her way, guessing at something. "Why ye might prefer it here."

"Do you?" she murmured, still not looking at him. "But, of course, you do."

He arched his brows, curious why she would say that. "You sound so certain."

She blinked a few times as though she'd been in a trance and finally glanced his way. "I'm sorry. I meant no offense. It just seems like you would enjoy such a place over worldly goods." She shook her head. "Forgive me, sometimes I just…"

Though he should probably leave it alone, considering they had only just met, when she trailed off, he couldn't help but prompt her along. "Sometimes, you just what?"

"Tend to think more than most, I suppose," she said more bluntly than he anticipated. "Or should I say get lost in my thoughts?"

That didn't surprise him, considering this place and the people around her. He would probably do the same. Yet, he sensed it went deeper. That it was related to whatever had happened to her.

"I would think getting lost in yer thoughts would help yer magic." He smiled, doing his best to make her feel normal, not less-than for being different than most. Because she *was* different. Wounded. Maybe even broken. "It undoubtedly lends to yer storytelling, aye?"

"Oh, that's just something I do for Duncan, Besse, and their mother." She blushed and picked an herb for her basket. "A means to give them a bit of happiness."

"'Tis nice." Though tempted to shift closer, he remained where he was lest someone happened along. "What brings them here, anyway?"

Her brow furrowed. A heavy frown marred her delicate features as she picked another plant. "They were given to my uncle after a border skirmish in payment for a debt owed."

He tensed. "So they are yer uncle's property now?"

"Yes," she replied tightly. "Which means they will eventually be split up. Likely sooner rather than later."

She didn't need to elaborate. He understood. *Bloody* Sassenach. He sighed and helped her pick plants, careful not to curse aloud and risk offending her. For not all English were bad. Cecille and Julianna most certainly were not, nor was Greer.

"Ye truly dinnae want them split apart, aye?" he asked.

"No." She shook her head sharply. "I most certainly do not."

"What *do* ye want then?" he asked, not merely to state the obvious but to see just how far she might go. How far she dared.

As it turned out, far indeed.

Chapter Six

Greer knew better than to bring Teagan to such a secluded spot, but when the chance arose to "escape" with her fictional hero, she just couldn't help herself. The temptation was too great.

It was foolish, though, and she knew it. Not just for her sake, but for his because he was Scottish. Therefore, he could be blamed for anything at any time, only for where he came from.

If that were not enough, now she hoped her hero would see through a quest she'd painted for him. But she simply couldn't help her strong emotions or passion when it came to this. More than that, she heard the determination in his voice when he'd spoken to Besse earlier. When he'd assured her, he would get her out of here.

"I want to smuggle all three of them out," she stated. "And it needs to happen before I'm married and no longer here to protect them."

Rather than look at her in shock, and say, "Ye're out of yer bloody mind!' a slow smile crept onto his face that made her stomach flutter. Almost as though she were going to swoon.

"At least your legs are more stable now that he's not outright smiling," Margery would have said, amused, teasing. "Can you imagine the mortification had they given out altogether? Had you just crumpled to the ground?"

She could. Very much so. She'd prayed they would keep her upright down the castle stairs, along the path leading here, then pretty much up to this moment. She'd never been so aware of a man in her life. Not just because of his substantial height and muscular build, either, but because of how gentle he'd been with her and Besse. How kind.

Then there was the way a dimple appeared in one cheek when he smiled. But then a roguish crooked smile would do that, wouldn't it? A sinful smile that kept her legs—or perhaps her knees specifically?—feeling rather weak.

"And just look at him helping you pick herbs," Margery would exclaim. "Can you imagine Bartholomew doing such a thing?"

No, never. But then Teagan and Bartholomew were remarkably different men. For example, her fiancé hated this very spot. Everything about nature. He had come here once with her, vowing never to do it again. According to him, it was nothing but filthy bathing water for the peasants.

"Though it willnae be easy," Teagan said, interrupting her reverie, "I agree that yer Scottish friends need to be gone from this place."

She nodded, relieved to hear him say it. "I know 'tis a lot to ask, but I have seen the fate of others before them and cannot stand to watch it happen again." Though tempted to move closer, to put her hand on his arm in a gesture of goodwill, she knew better. "I will do anything you need of me. Anything at all." She shook her head. "I care nothing of my welfare after you get them out of here."

"But yer ma will." He frowned, not seeming to care they had only just met. "As do I." Though it seemed he wanted to say one thing, he hesitated and said another. "Whatever comes of it all, I will find a way to get them out of here, Greer."

Whatever comes of it all?

As if there were more to this than what she asked of him?

"It sounds like your Scottish friends are not the only thing he wants to smuggle out of here," Margery would hedge, smirking at her. "Perhaps you will be riding off into the sunset after all?"

"Do not think like that," she whispered, cursing it the moment she said it, mainly because Teagan looked at her curiously again. When he responded, she realized he replied the way he did on purpose. That he was trying to keep her from feeling bad about talking to herself.

"I *will* think like that," he said. "For they dinnae deserve the life they currently live nor the one that surely lies ahead."

"Thank you," she said softly, genuinely grateful. She was about to say more when he put a finger to his lips that she stay quiet, looked back the way they had come, and slowly unsheathed his dirk.

As it happened, her mother appeared moments later. She swore she saw a flash of approval in her eyes that Greer and Teagan were together before her expression switched to one of surprise.

"My apologies." Mother stopped short. "Was I intruding?"

"Of course not," Greer said too quickly, feeling guilty when she should not. "Why would you be intruding?"

Her mother glanced between them curiously before she relented. "True. 'Tis not as if I stumbled upon a secret tryst."

"A *tryst*?" Greer exclaimed, stunned she would say such a thing.

"Is it me, or is there amusement in your mother's eyes?" Margery would tease. "Perhaps even, dare I say, hope?"

There best not be.

But what if there was? What would that mean?

She frowned at her mother and Teagan, wondering if she imagined things. For Mother envisioning her with Teagan was a preposterous notion. An outright impossible one.

"Yes, dear, a tryst," her mother replied, waving it away as though she hadn't meant to say it.

Good. Enough of that.

Yet almost as an afterthought, her mother continued, mortifying Greer more by the moment. "But then, a romantic tryst betwixt you and Teagan would be impossible at this juncture, considering you only just met."

Teagan muttered something indiscernible under his breath, then saved the day.

"Yer daughter is too much of a lady for that, Cecille." He sheathed his blade and shook his head. "Even jesting about such is inappropriate, aye?"

"Is it, though?" Margery would wonder, mirth dancing in her eyes again. "Because I think we both know being a lady around the likes of him is a struggle."

Was it ever. Not just because of the desire he invoked, but because of the freedom she felt around him. She had no idea why, either. Only that it drove her to bring him here, to begin with. A bold move, considering she was engaged to be married.

Her cheeks warmed at the thought of what might have happened had her mother not come along. How their hands may have mistakenly brushed when they reached for the same herb. How their gazes would have connected and lingered. Caught in the moment, he might have brushed his fingers along her cheek. Trailed them down her neck. Along her heaving chest.

No, no, that's not how he would have gone about it at all. Instead, his gaze would linger on her lips, his desire unmistakable, his need for her undeniable. She would lick her lips, tempting him to imagine what else she might do with her mouth. Then he would lick his lips…

"Enough with the lips," Margery would cut in, rolling her eyes. "Just kiss the man already!"

"Are you all right, darling?" her mother said, interrupting her thoughts. "You seem a bit red in the face."

"Do I?" She fanned her face with her hand, feigning innocence. "'Tis a rather warm afternoon."

In truth, it was fairly cool.

Thankfully, her mother went along with it, however knowing her gaze.

"'*Tis* rather warm." Mother eyed the location, her gaze sentimental. "You always did love this spot, daughter."

She wondered if her mother recalled the numerous times she, Greer, Julianna, and their father had picnicked here.

"Yes, 'tis a nice spot," she replied, not sure what else to say. How she truly felt.

Although she loved this area, something about her mother being here right now left a sour taste in her mouth. Her presence reminded Greer how she'd left and never returned. How they all did.

"I should get back," she murmured, forcing the words out when she would rather flee without saying anything. Flee before she grew too upset and said things she might regret.

"Must you?" Mother's pained gaze turned her way. "Why not stay and enjoy the view with me? We need not talk if you prefer the silence."

"No." She said goodbye to Teagan in passing. "I must get back."

Fortunately, her mother didn't stop her, and she made it to the kitchens without seeing anyone else, most especially Bartholomew. The children's mother, Ada, was the only one she ran into just outside the door.

Greer gestured at the basket and smiled. "Some extra herbs for cooking if you need them."

A small woman with bright red hair and fiery blue eyes, Ada was like bright sunlight dimmed by storm clouds. Repressed and unable to shine as she should. One could see how lovely she was, but like Greer, she was bound by those around her. Imprisoned in a life where she didn't belong. That was probably why they got along so well. Or, for that matter, why Greer smiled at all.

"Ye know I dinnae need more herbs," Ada eyed the basket, then glanced in the direction of the river with amusement. "But then I imagine ye needed a good reason to tromp off alone with our handsome new arrival."

"I was not *tromping*," she defended.

"Aye, more like floating on thin air." Ada chuckled before she grew serious. "'Twas good seeing ye smile like that."

She'd been smiling? "You make me smile."

"Aye, but not nearly enough." Ada's eyes twinkled. "And not nearly like that."

"I did not realize I was," she murmured before something occurred to her, and she frowned. If Ada saw them so clearly, who else might have?"

"'Twas only me who saw ye, friend," Ada said, guessing Greer's unspoken concerns. But then she had a gift for that sort of thing. "I think yer bigger concern should be how much ye spoke with Margery on yer stroll." She narrowed her eyes and cocked her head. "Though mayhap 'twould not be such a bad thing for the braw lad to meet her upfront."

"I…she…" Greer cleared her throat, knowing better than to claim she talked to herself to Ada. "I spoke with her very little."

"What does she think of Teagan?"

"You know his name?"

"Aye, I know everything that happens around here, mistress, and well ye know it." Having obviously talked to her children, she winked. "Even about yer warrior-hero."

God love them; they were chatty children.

"Margery likes him." She gave Ada a look she couldn't misinterpret. "And it just so happens he *is* a hero."

"Och," Ada murmured, understanding what Greer implied. For, Besse would have told her why Teagan was their "warrior-hero." Hope flashed in her eyes before they dulled with resolve. "'Tis nice to think he might be our savior, friend." She shook her head. "But unless he has an army at his disposal, 'tis impossible as far as I can see."

"Whatever he has," she lowered her voice, lest others overhear, "he seems determined. As if he wants to help no matter what it takes."

"Then, we can only hope he has an army backing him." Though emotion simmered in her eyes, Ada stayed strong. "I know yer uncle intends to get coin for my children. As to his plans for me, I think we both know where that will lead."

She did, and didn't like it one bit. The way he looked at Ada lately was telling.

"I will speak with Teagan again soon," Greer assured, "and find out how he intends to go about things. If, perhaps, he has fighting men who might help."

When Ada nodded and looked at her hesitantly, Greer frowned. "What is it?"

"I was thinking mayhap ye should come along, too, if he gets us out of here."

"I could never," she began before Ada cut her off and whispered in her ear exactly why she might want to reconsider *never*.

Chapter Seven

"SHE'S FURIOUS AT me." Cecille lowered to the bench after Greer left. Her shoulders slumped. "And she has every right to be."

"Aye, mayhap," Teagan conceded, joining her. "But only because she doesnae understand everything that happened. She doesnae know ye went to Scotland for treasure to start a new life and waited to come for her because ye had no choice."

"Did I not, though?" She frowned and shook her head. "I could have found a way here sooner. I could have..."

She trailed off, knowing full well it went the only way it could have. They had needed Edmund's help, and he hadn't been available any sooner.

"Ye need to be upfront with Greer as soon as possible," he counseled. "To give her hope, if nothing else."

It had taken everything in him not to tell Greer what he knew. To make it clear, she would not, so long as he lived and breathed, remain behind if she took part in getting her friends out of here. He would not have her harmed by Bartholomew and Randolph.

While Randolph was no good, he suspected the man she was about to marry was even worse. Teagan might be damaged from the war, but he was still an excellent judge of character.

Men like Bartholomew found their self-worth from degrading those they felt beneath them, which would, undoubtedly, apply to his wife. More so her than anyone. Worse yet, he highly suspected, having come across monsters like him in the war, the bulk of her punishment would take place in the bedchamber.

"You want Greer gone from here, don't you?" Cecille said softly, pulling him from his thoughts. "You like her?"

"I do." Rather than satisfy her romantic notions, he remained practical. "I think we understand each other and would get along well."

"Understand each other, is it?" Mirth flickered in Cecille's eyes. "What precisely do you understand about her? That she's in need of saving? Or perhaps that she's as haunted as you? Because surely it's not her beauty, gentle nature, or kind ways."

Rather than admit to the attraction she hinted at, he kept things where they needed to be. Or specifically, filled her in on the Scottish mother and bairns he intended to save.

"I dinnae know how I'm going to go about it yet, but I will see Greer's wishes through," he vowed. "And I willnae leave her behind if she decides to take part in it but insists on staying. I willnae leave her behind to be punished by these men if they learn of her role in it."

"Nor should you," Cecille exclaimed. "No matter what she says!" She shook her head. "She always did have an overly kind heart. Especially toward those in my brother's employ and the unfortunate Scots who ended up under his care."

"Is that what ye would call it?" Wee Besse had been gaunt. Undernourished. "*Care*?"

"My apologies. That was the wrong word." Cecille squeezed his hand and ground her jaw. "Randolph has never cared for anyone but himself and his ambitions. I used to help Greer steal food from the kitchens for those in need. It seems she has not changed."

Thank God. He liked her just the way she was. Not to say he wasn't curious what had happened to make her talk to herself so often. Mayhap she merely suffered loneliness, but he suspected it was something more.

"Or should I say Greer has not changed entirely," Cecille said on a sigh, thinking along the same lines as him. But how could she not, being Greer's mother?

"You may find her," Cecille struggled to find the right words, "a touch different than most women."

"Mayhap." He shrugged. "But then 'tis safe to say the same thing about me, aye?"

"Perhaps." Cecille gave him the sort of compassionate look his own mother might have given were she still alive. "In my opinion, there is something to be said for those who walk their own paths. Who battle demons most of us can only imagine."

He knew from what Cecille and Julianna had said that Greer had gone through something difficult. Something he saw clearly when he looked at her. While tempted to ask Cecille what it was, he would rather ask Greer directly if the occasion ever arose. Or better yet, that she told him without being asked. To trust him enough.

"We cannae leave Greer with the likes of Bartholomew." Talking about his own demons wasn't going to happen. At least not with Cecille. He could be blunt about what Greer faced if she stayed, though. "He isnae the sort she should be marrying."

"No," Cecille agreed. "The issue, however, is how to make her see that. Or, if I know my Greer, how to convince her to go back on her word to him. Even if that word was my brother's."

"Ye dinnae think she will want to get away from Bartholomew?" He frowned, troubled. "Despite how he treats her?"

"'Tis impossible to know." Cecille shook her head. "Greer has always been the sort to honor her word no matter what. Even with one marriage behind her that I suspect was not good, she would not refuse a second if she already committed."

"I didnae realize she was married before."

"Nor I." She sighed again. "Rest assured, I intend to speak with my brother about it. What sort of horror my daughter has faced already." She stood and held out her elbow to him. "Until then, let us get back to the castle so that I might see to business and ponder a way to get not just my daughter out of here but her newfound friends."

He wasn't surprised she'd decided to save them all. Though Cecille would never admit it, Greer came by her soft heart naturally.

After he and Cecille went their separate ways at the castle, he ran into Edmund in the courtyard.

"I wondered where you got off to, friend." Edmund clasped Teagan's shoulder and urged him to join him for a ride before supper. As they headed for the stables, he flicked a bit of dust off his sleeve. A signal that they would talk more when they were alone.

Teagan eyed Edmund curiously when he turned away the stable boy's offer to ready the horses. He realized why when he spied the wee lad who'd been with Greer peek around the corner, then pull back.

"You need not be shy, laddie," Edmund called out, winking at Teagan. "Why do you think I ready my own horse?"

The boy's freckled face peeked out again, unsure before he rallied his courage and sidled along the wall, keeping to the shadows. Edmund introduced them when the lad was close enough, then asked him his name.

"It doesnae matter." The boy took them in warily before he straightened and notched his chin. "I come on a mission of utmost importance."

Teagan couldn't help a small grin, suspecting this had to do with Besse. "Do ye then?"

"I do." The lad peered at them through a heavy shock of dark hair. "'Tis about my lasses."

"Your lasses?" Edmund's brows shot up. "And who are they?"

"I think ye know who." The bairn stood straighter still and narrowed his eyes. "I think ye both do."

Intrigued, Edmund crossed his arms over his chest and cocked his head. "Actually, I do not."

"Duncan," came a sharp voice from the back entrance. A lovely redhead appeared and gestured at the boy to join her. "Come along now." Her wary gaze flickered from Teagan to Edmund and lingered a moment. "Leave the good men be, aye?"

"But—"

"*Now.*"

Before they had a chance to tell her all was well, that she need not worry, she and Duncan were gone, clearly well practiced at moving fast.

"Now there was a bonnie lass if ever I saw one," Edmund praised as they saddled their horses. "What was that all about? It sounded like—"

"Aye, verra bonnie," Teagan agreed, cutting his friend off before he said another word.

As soon as they were beyond the castle and alone in the woodland, the conversation continued.

"This has turned into a rescue mission, indeed." Edmund grinned in anticipation. "So we are to get the wee lassie we just saw and her children to safety?"

"Aye," Teagan confirmed. "At least I am." He shook his head. "This is not something ye need do, Edmund. 'Tis awful to burn bridges so close to home, aye?"

Edmund gestured flippantly in the direction of the castle, referring to Randolph and Bartholomew. "If you are referring to the bridges of those two fools back there, then might I single-handedly light the flames."

"They are intolerable," he agreed, relieved to know he had his friend's help. Even so. "Ye ken, if ye're caught, it could mean yer title? Yer estate? Everything?"

"'Twould not be the first time I was coinless," Edmund replied, referring to their long years at war. "Worry naught, friend. I would find my way."

"Mayhap stay on at MacLauchlin Castle afterward?" he prompted, hedging. "Ye've long been like a brother to me. 'Twould do my heart good to have ye as close as my blood brothers."

"We will have to see where things lead." As a rule, Edmund was a drifter, preferring to go where the next adventure took him. "Not to say I won't stay on for a time, depending on how things go."

"Aye, then." He tilted his head in question. "So, what did ye wish to speak with me about before we ran into Duncan and his ma?"

"Things I suspect you've already surmised but bear talking about considering you are set to marry Greer." Edmund's gaze darkened. "Whilst Randolph is certainly not a good man, you realize Bartholomew is something else altogether, yes?"

"Aye." By Edmund's tone, trouble was already brewing. "What worries ye, friend?"

"Besides Bartholomew's general hatred of Scots and his obvious jealousy of you," Edmund replied, "a great deal." He shook his head. "Not only his questionable dealings with Randolph but the way he speaks of Greer. What we both know he intends for her."

"Did he confirm such then?" Teagan exclaimed.

"Without going into detail about what you and I both know he will do to her," Edmund frowned, "he claims she needs "special help," as he puts it."

"*Special* help?" he ground out, clenching his hands. "What kind of special help?"

"The kind reserved for lasses not right in the head." Edmund's expression soured like he had a bad taste in his mouth. "It seems many here consider Greer daft. They say she talks to phantoms more often than not. So Bartholomew assured Randolph he would see to such. Once they are married, he will set things straight in her mind once and for all."

"What does he bloody mean to do to her?" Though he already had a good idea. "He'll *set things straight*, my arse. He willnae be going anywhere near her!"

If it was within his power, he'd get her out of here right now, so she was no longer subjected to these people and their foul opinions.

"Greer isnae crazed but has lived through a nightmare," he said through clenched teeth. "She's coping the only way she knows how. Trying to survive in an unaccepting place, surrounded by men who only want her to serve their purposes."

Forget merely saving her. If Teagan had his way, he'd gut Bartholomew and shove his entrails straight up his…

"I know," Edmund concurred, interrupting his dark thoughts.

His friend grasped his shoulder and squeezed until Teagan glanced his way.

"You have my word we will get her out of here, my friend." He squeezed one more time, much like he'd done during difficult times in the war. "Do you understand, Teagan? We *will* get her out. The only way to do that, though, is to keep your wits about you and play their game for now." He shook his head. "If you cannot control your rage, all *will* be lost."

"Aye," he managed.

"Aye?" Edmund switched to his brogue. "If ye keep her needs ahead of yers, which I know ye can, there isnae anything stopping us. They are nae nearly bright enough to stop us if we put our heads together."

"Nay." Time to use his God-given mind rather than let his emotions get the better of him. "Which means we best get to plotting, aye?"

"I already have." A smile crept onto Edmund's face. "And here's what I think…"

Chapter Eight

"MY BAIRNS JUST cannae stay out of trouble," Ada muttered yet again, shaking her head as she tended to Greer's hair. "Getting into mischief at every turn!" Her eyes rounded. "And that big Sassenach had the nerve to eye me over whilst making nice with a laddie ye know he has no use for."

"You mean the big, handsome Englishman?" Greer grinned if for no other reason than it was nice to have the tables turned. Because her friend was clearly smitten. "I believe his name is Edmund, and I'm sure if he's Teagan's brother, he's not all that bad."

"Right, because ye go *way* back with yer warrior-hero, so ye can speak to how his kin should be," Ada mocked, looking skyward. The corner of her mouth curled up ever-so-slightly. "Though I *do* like yer sense of familiarity with yer future betrothed."

"Stop that," she chastised, standing before Ada could fiddle with her hair anymore. Somewhere between the kitchens earlier and getting ready to eat, her friend had taken to calling Teagan that. "Bartholomew is my future husband, and well you know it."

More often than not, lately, Ada filled in for her maid, and she much preferred it. Even at moments like this when her friend spoke of the impossible. Of things that would never come to be. Oh, but it was nice to dream, though, wasn't it? She might not know Teagan, but she sensed him a far better man than Bartholomew. One who seemed to genuinely enjoy her company rather than merely tolerating her or wanting to get betwixt her thighs.

"Ye never know," Ada chimed, adding a veil to Greer's hair before she got away. "I cannae imagine yer warrior-hero riding off into the sunset without ye."

"Your children really are chatty," Greer muttered but couldn't help a small smile. "But lovely nonetheless."

"Aye, wee bairns who want to see ye happy." Ada cupped her cheeks and grew serious. "As do I, ye know?" She shook her head. "Which means if I have a chance of escaping all this, then ye do, too."

"How do you imagine that happening with men like my uncle and Bartholomew around?" She sighed and stepped away. "If that were not enough, I gave my word."

"Did ye?" Ada cocked her head and narrowed her eyes. "Did ye actually commit to marrying Bartholomew, because I dinnae think it happened that way. Nay, ye were *told*. Given no choice." She gripped Greer's shoulders and met her eyes. "If all that isnae enough, 'tis important ye listen to what I shared earlier. What I learned from Bartholomew's cook."

"Which could very well be rumor." Or so she prayed, for it was hard to believe anyone so depraved. Which said something considering the atrocities she'd seen. "And whilst no, I did not actually say yes to Bartholomew, it was agreed upon, and that is how things are done."

Did she wish it otherwise? With all her heart. But by not denying it or saying no, to her mind and in God's eyes, she believed her word *was* given. That she had an obligation to fulfill.

"You are being foolish," Margery would have said. "You never wanted this, nor was your permission given. After what you learned about Bartholomew earlier, the only thing at work in your mind now is the devil because God does not approve."

"You cannot possibly know that," she muttered under her breath.

"Bloody hell, aye," Ada said, knowing full well when Greer was elsewhere in her mind. More so, that Margery could often be her voice of reason. "Ye tell Margery, I agree."

She waved her friend off and headed for the door. "You don't even know what she said."

"I dinnae need to," Ada called after her. "She's right, and ye should heed her!"

Getting her thoughts in order again is what she needed to do. She loved Ada, but the woman could get her mind going in circles as quickly as Margery sometimes. A mere phantom of her imagination.

"No, not a phantom." She leaned against the corridor wall, closed her eyes, and whispered, "I'm sorry, Margery. You will *never* be a phantom. Not so long as I live." She shook her head and bit back tears. "I promise you are still right here. Still with me—"

"Dear Lord, woman, what are you doing?" came Bartholomew's exasperated voice from behind her.

When Greer opened her eyes, she swore she saw Teagan watching her before he vanished into the shadows. Oddly, being caught in such a vulnerable position by him didn't bother her. Being caught by Bartholomew, however, made her feel unstable and ashamed.

"I'm taking a moment to reflect and pray," she lied far too readily. But if she didn't, it would mean suffering his disgust, and she was in no mood for it. Mustering a halfhearted smile, she looked his way. "Good eve, Bartholomew."

"We shall see," he replied dryly before eyeing her over with his usual predatory gleam. "You will have to take special care to keep your eyes averted this eve, love, for there is a beast amongst us."

"A dashing Scot he's horribly jealous of," Margery exclaimed, suddenly seeming closer to her than ever. "A man that puts him to shame."

Relieved to hear her again, Greer bit back a smile and managed a respectful nod to Bartholomew. "But of course."

"You see the Scotsman for what he is, then?" He preceded her down the stairs. "You understand that, despite his façade, he is filthy and wild?" He stopped and glanced over his shoulder sternly. "That he is half-human if that?"

Half-human? That was a bit much, even for Bartholomew.

Such was ignorance and hatred, though.

"Can you blame him?" Margery muttered. "'Tis not easy being such a lowly coward, not to mention a monster. Remember, evil will say and do whatever it takes to feel superior."

Whilst more tempted than usual to repeat what she was thinking, now was not the time to risk getting backhanded. Not when she needed to get Ada and her children out. So, as much as she detested her silence, she merely lowered her head in what seemed like compliance.

As usual, at this hour, the great hall was busy. People came and went, some eating, others socializing. The family's dining area in an adjacent solar was set in finery, not only for Bartholomew's visit but Edmund's. There was no length her uncle would not go to impress them.

"Welcome!" Randolph's bald head gleamed beneath the chandeliers, just begging to be hit with dripping wax. "So good of you to join us."

Ignoring Greer, he urged Bartholomew to join everyone in front of the fire for wine and ale. Her mother looked fetching in a simple, dark crimson gown. Edmund seemed ever mysterious with a keen eye on the fire as if plotting his next step in a play only he understood. Dressed mostly in black, Teagan struck her the fierce, brooding hero just waiting to steal her away into the night.

"So no more gallantly riding off into the sunset?" Margery quipped. "Though I do rather like a dark and dangerous escape."

She bit back another smile, lowered her head, and averted her eyes when curtseying to everyone.

"Do hold your chin up like a lady," Bartholomew muttered under his breath. "You look like an ignorant fool. 'Tis insulting."

"And you look like someone who should drop to his knees and beg God's forgiveness, you awful man," she *should* have shot back but didn't. Now wasn't the time or place. She lifted her chin, tempted to do it defiantly. Moreover, she was tempted to look right at Teagan just to irk

Bartholomew. Of course, she didn't. No need to turn his ever-growing insecurities the Scotsman's way.

Instead, she looked at her mother, only to see a flash of pity and anger. She was an embarrassment, wasn't she? Mother was ashamed. A woman should look a man in the eyes out of respect. In her world, though, with Bartholomew and Randolph, it was quite the opposite. They preferred her submissive.

"Are you sure your mother is ashamed?" She heard the frown in Margery's voice. "I would hazard to say any shame she feels is for letting you down. And her anger? Solely at your uncle and the buffoon you are determined to marry."

"I never said I was determined."

"Well, you never said otherwise either, did you?"

"You look beautiful, Greer," her mother said. She moved to her side. "Really, so very lovely."

Did she? It was impossible to know since Bartholomew never praised her.

"Who cares what he thinks?" Margery would mutter. "I'm far more interested in what the Scotsman trying so hard not to stare at you thinks. For I'm fairly certain he finds you—"

"Thank you," she replied to her mother, cutting off any more talk of handsome Scots finding her attractive. "You look very fetching as well."

Her mother nodded in thanks before everyone commenced to chatting about things of little relevance. As was expected of her, and despite Mother trying to keep her in the conversation, she faded into the background as always, accepting the role of being ignored by men.

"Not Teagan, though," Margery whispered into her mind. "He might not be looking directly at you, but your warrior-hero is keeping an eye on you, wishing you would talk."

She ignored her friend's fanciful notions, relieved when Alfred joined them and faded into the background beside her. He smiled kindly and nodded hello, then kept quiet for fear of being mocked.

Whilst they rarely spoke in general, she knew him a kind soul. More of a man than her uncle and Bartholomew would ever be.

"'Tis nice to have visitors," she commented, wondering not for the first time, why they didn't talk more.

"'T-tis," he agreed, looking at her with hope as he sometimes did.

"Because you are his cousin, and he cares about you," Margery would say. "He worries about you."

She ignored her friend, grateful when the chaplain said the evening prayers and food was served, including pigeon pie, carrots, and peas as well as capers, nuts, and sliced bread. What did Margery know? Little when it came to this.

"Do not fool yourself, Greer," Margery echoed as bowls of water were placed in front of everyone for washing their hands. "You and I both know why Alfred—"

"Tell us about your clan, Scotsman," Bartholomew said, interrupting her thoughts. There was no missing the disdain in his voice. Nor that the tasty, upper crust of the bread was served to Edmund and her fiancé, yet none to Teagan despite his status as a guest.

"There is little to tell other than we dinnae support David II." Teagan's brow furrowed. His eyes flared with anger. "If not for him and our troublesome alliance with France, our clan would be much better off nowadays." He shook his head. "Our supposed king has done us no favors."

"No." Edmund frowned and perked a brow at Randolph. "As I said before, 'twas with good reason I finally saw the error of my ways. That I returned home to my father and righted old wrongs."

Randolph nodded, near-genuine sympathy in his eyes. "That took great courage, my lord. Great courage, to be sure. And England is grateful for it." He raised his mug to Bartholomew and Edmund. "Thankful for good men like you that make this country superior!"

"Because it could not possibly be England's weak, pitiful women." Mother arched her brows at her brother. "Now could it?"

"I never said *pitiful*." Randolph's reddening nose gave away the several cups of wine he'd already had. He swigged half his glass, then raised it higher. "As to the rest, 'tis all details as long as one cuts a lovely figure."

Bartholomew raised his glass higher in agreement, then downed the entire thing. Meanwhile, Edmund and Teagan barely touched their wine as the excruciating supper wore on. Randolph and Bartholomew acted like they always did when in their cups. Obnoxious and pretentious, more often than not, jesting silently about the useless Scots in their equally useless country.

"One has to wonder why we English keep trying to take it for our own then," Margery would pipe up, sarcastically. "Certainly not for the revenue it provides us in taxes, nor its natural resources."

"Is it me, or do you get the sense he wants to fight back?" Greer asked her. "That he actually takes issue with such comments?"

"Who?" Margery would reply before her tone grew knowing. "Ah, you must mean your warrior-hero. No, I do not wonder at all because I think him as mysterious as his good friend, Edmund."

"Surely not."

"Oh, yes." She could almost see Margery contemplating the men. "I would say them sympathetic not to England but Scotland and here for heroic purposes indeed!"

Were they? Could it be true?

She glanced at her mother. If that were the case, that would mean her flesh and blood were likely in cohorts with them. Which would make sense considering her sister Julianna had remained in Scotland.

The possibility of so many traitors amid them weighed on her mind as the night wore on. Eventually, dining turned into after-supper drinks for the men. By that point, her uncle and Bartholomew were well in their cups, and she was glad to escape.

Or so she thought when she slipped out the back of the castle alone a short while later.

Chapter Nine

TEAGAN WANTED TO roar at the moon like the wild beast these Sassenach thought him but kept his rage contained for one reason alone. Greer and his ever-growing need to get her out of here. He was galled by how poorly she was treated. How repressed these monsters had made her.

He sat against a tree overlooking the river, inhaling and exhaling slowly, trying to remain calm. Controlled. Rein in his demons. But it wasn't easy.

During supper, he'd wanted to whip a dagger into Randolph's forehead far too many times to count. When he wasn't fantasizing about that, he'd envisioned driving his sword into Bartholomew's groin and pinning him to the chair. Then and only then would he finally enjoy some Sassenach wine and watch the lout slowly bleed out.

Greer did not deserve this. None of it. He would have given anything to simply enjoy her company tonight. To admire her openly and get to know her better. To mayhap, if he was capable, make her smile. Even laugh. Not just once, either. He had known her but a day and wanted to see her laugh all the time.

As if Greer manifested from his thoughts, she melted out of the darkness and stood at the shoreline. Her gown trailed on the ground, her silhouette stunning. She'd removed her veil, and her dark-as-night hair shimmered in the moonlight.

It had taken a great deal of effort keeping his eyes off of her earlier when she came downstairs. Her hair had been pulled back and veiled, but tendrils trailed down her neck, dusting her delicate collarbone. For the first time in longer than he could remember feeling anything for a woman, he wanted to reach out and follow those wisps of hair. Touch her soft skin. Enjoy a woman for the warmth she offered rather than the coldness he still carried from that fateful day so long ago.

He went to say something, to let her know he was there but stopped when he heard Cecille moments before she appeared.

"Greer," she said in greeting. "I did not expect to find you here."

Despite the darkness, he saw Greer tense. "I should not be."

She went to leave, but Cecille caught her arm. "Please do not go. We need to talk."

He frowned, wondering what he should do. While certainly stealthy, they were far too close for him to leave without making a sound. On the other hand, he hated to disturb much-needed time alone between them. Unfortunately, he had no choice but to stand and clear his throat, making his presence known.

Cecille's eyebrows swept up. "Teagan?"

"Aye, apologies." He nodded at them in passing. "I was enjoying a wee bit o' fresh air but will leave ye be."

"No," Cecille and Greer exclaimed at the same time.

"I will walk back with you," Greer said, clearly trying to get away from her mother.

"Yes, but not yet," Cecille said, stopping them in their tracks. "First, the three of us must talk frankly."

Ah, so it was time to share all. Part of which, as Cecille only revealed a few hours ago, included her "bargaining chip." It turned out the jewel she'd mentioned before was worth far more than he imagined. He understood why she hesitated to use it but was grateful she had in the end. That the lives of not just Greer but her Scottish friends meant so much.

For this jewel changed everything.

Greer glanced from Teagan to Cecille and frowned. "Here? Now? In the middle of the forest?"

"You mean at your favorite spot that brings you comfort." Cecille gestured to the bench. Her tone broached no room for argument. "Could you please sit so we might discuss our plan, daughter?"

"Whose plan?" Greer asked, not sitting beside Teagan. She might cower to men who meant to crush her, but it seemed she could stand up to her mother just fine. A mother who, sadly, only meant the best for her. But he supposed if she could manage to stand up to at least one person, Cecille would gladly volunteer.

"Our plan to get you and your friends out of here." Cecille glanced from the bench to Greer. "You really should sit for this, dear."

"I'm fine." Yet she gripped the back of the bench, without doubt, worried they might not be able to free her friends. She glanced at Teagan, seeming to find more comfort in looking at him. "As you know, I will do whatever it takes."

"Ironic, you would say that," Cecille said softly. "For whatever it takes is right in front of you."

Greer narrowed her eyes at her mother. "What do you mean?"

"She means me, Greer," he said before Cecille had a chance to respond. "You and I are what it will take to get your friends out of here safely."

Though he loathed going about things in this fashion, Cecille felt it was the only way to get Greer out, too. Apparently, she'd sought out the children's mother, Ada, so she knew the truth of it. Cecille would honor a word she'd never actually given to Bartholomew. She would continue being Randolph's pawn out of a moral and ethical code he by no means adhered to himself.

So, though Teagan would have preferred to be upfront and honest with Greer, her safety meant more than what she ultimately thought of him.

"Agree to marry me instead of Bartholomew," he continued, "and I will see yer friends free of this place."

She couldn't know that he would have done it either way. Rather, she needed to believe she had no choice if she hoped to save them.

Greer's stunned, perhaps even hurt gaze lingered on him for a moment before she replied, however stunted. "I told you..." When her gaze drifted to the river, he knew she was retreating into the safety of her mind. "I told you I would do anything."

No questioning it. Just acceptance and compliance.

Relief flashed in Cecille's eyes. "So you will marry Teagan?"

"I will do whatever it takes," Greer whispered. She cleared her throat and, at last, sank onto the bench beside him, almost as if she had no choice. As if she was but a possession sold to one man and then another. Defeated and hopeless.

He wasn't any man, though. And she had a great deal of hope ahead of her.

Just as troubled by Greer's behavior as he was, Cecille inhaled deeply before finally telling her daughter the whole story. Not just about the family jewels she and Greer's father had stolen, but the pact Teagan had made with his brothers to restore their clan.

"So, my dowry is a piece of this fortune." Greer's shoulders sank. "The other, this main jewel that uncle wants, has convinced him to take me from Bartholomew and give me to Teagan."

Not a question but a lackluster statement.

"Aye," he replied when it seemed too difficult for Cecille. He explained how they had left the jewel at Edmund's holding in case they were searched upon arrival. "Edmund will ride back to his estate and retrieve the gem. Then, once your uncle has it in hand, he will let us go."

"A jewel that proves he's related to the King of England," she said softly, "which will make my marriage unnecessary. After all, it would confirm his royalty, earning him the prestige he's so desperate for."

"That's right," Cecille confirmed. "So he will no longer need you."

In a thousand lifetimes, he would have never thought someone like King Edward III, the man responsible for so much Scottish bloodshed, capable of relations like these women, but apparently, it was true.

Greer remained silent for what seemed an eternity but was likely only a few moments. She sighed and put her head down, redirecting her submissive behavior effortlessly from Bartholomew to him. "May I go now, Teagan?"

While he might ken the necessity behind all this, there was no reason for him to behave like other men had.

"Only if ye wish, lass." He wanted to rest his hand over hers or, at the very least, touch her in reassurance but knew it was too soon. "Though I would much rather ye stay and spend time with yer good ma."

Now that she understood why her mother hadn't come back straight away, he assumed she would want to spend time with her. Then again, though Cecille had made clear she hadn't abandoned Greer, she *had* just supported her daughter marrying another without any real choice in the matter. So it wasn't all that surprising when Greer requested to leave.

Her eyes remained lowered. "If 'tis just the same, I would rather get some rest."

"Of course, darling." Cecille started forward. "Let me walk you back."

"Please, no." Greer shook her head and glanced at Teagan, asking his permission. "If 'tis all right, I would rather walk back alone."

"Aye, lass, whatever ye wish."

"Thank you." She curtsied and vanished almost as quickly as she came.

Though tempted to make sure she made it back safely, he sensed she did this sort of thing often at night and knew her way around just fine.

"Bloody *hell.*" He braced his elbows on his knees and hung his head. "This isnae fair to her." He scowled at Cecille, who stared forlornly after Greer. "She thinks me but another man who means to own her."

He realized even as he said it how that sounded, and Cecille took notice.

"Well, you are, are you not?" Cecille arched a brow. "Or so that's how things appear." She sat beside him, her gaze compassionate. "However distanced you mean to keep your heart from all this, feeling nothing for Greer's circumstances is impossible for a man like you. So I'm sorry your journey with her had to start out this way. That..." She clenched her teeth, grappling with anger. "That you could not give her the choice she so rightly deserves for once in her life."

"I will, though," he vowed, never so certain of anything. "I will give her the same choice Malcolm gave Isabella, with or without her dowry. After we marry, I will let her go if that is her desire."

"You will have her dowry," Cecille said softly, surprising him with her vehemence. "And God willing, in the end, her heart, too."

That, as he told her yet again, was not something he sought. Even so, as he lay in bed later that night, he found himself wondering what it would feel like to open his heart to a lass. He'd never done it, so had nothing to draw on.

Before he and his brothers went off to war, he'd been more like Malcolm. Lighthearted and flirtatious, enjoying lasses aplenty but never falling in love. After that, the years of battling made love seem more and more improbable. That day in the village made it downright impossible. He was too changed. Too disenchanted. Since then, he barely lay with a lass, much less entertained the idea of anything more.

Now he was curious or at least intrigued.

He intended to put Edmund's time away to good use and get to know Greer better. Which, as he discovered the next day, would not always go so smoothly.

Chapter Ten

GREER TOSSED AND turned all night, barely sleeping a wink. Eventually, she gave up, sat by the window overlooking the courtyard, and watched the sun crest the horizon.

"I understand why you are upset," Margery would say. "But is this not what you wanted? Does the idea of marrying Teagan instead of Bartholomew not appeal to you?"

"You know it does," she'd reply. "But not like this. Not told rather than asked."

When a light rap came at the door, she called out that Ada could enter, not surprised to see her friend up so early.

"Good morn," Greer said in greeting. "I would ask how you knew I was awake, but know better."

"Aye, I heard ye looked glum upon yer return to the castle last night, so figured ye'd have a restless night." Ada sat beside her, concerned. "What happened? Because I know yer future betrothed and mother made their way to the river as well."

Though she might be out of sorts, there was no reason for her friend to be. So she squeezed Ada's hand and mustered a smile. "I have good news."

She filled her in on their plan.

Though wary, hope flared in Ada's eyes. Yet, instead of focusing on her own impending freedom, she remained concerned about Greer's discontent.

"So ye're to marry yer warrior-hero after all. That's good!" As usual, Ada figured out Greer quickly enough. Her smile wavered, and she cocked her head. "'Tis not quite the story ye spun in yer mind, though, aye?"

Of course, it wasn't. In any love story, a man would marry a woman for love, not her dowry. She would be worth more than the coin that came with her or, in this case, jewels. Greer didn't voice such, though, because it was too unrealistic a desire to bother complaining about.

And truly, *did* such love exist beyond a tale?

"No," Greer admitted. "When I envisioned this, I was not told to marry another man nor forced to break my good word." She tried to look at the bright side. "Though I will admit this situation has a better outlook than marrying Bartholomew."

"A thousand times over," Margery would mutter. "So stop brooding."

"Bloody hell right, this situation is better," Ada exclaimed. "I have known Teagan but a day and can say, without hesitation, he's a far better man than the one ye were going to marry." Empathetic, she rested her hand over Greer's. "I know more than most how difficult it is not having control over yer own life. How hard it is to be told what ye can and cannae do." She shook her head. "But trust me, this turn of events is likely the best thing that's happened to ye in a verra long time, Greer."

Ada paused as if gathering her thoughts. "I have always had a keen sense about people, so I can tell ye, with near certainty, ye'll find a good man in Teagan. I suspect ye two have more in common than ye think. I sense there's..." She tilted her head as if listening to somebody no one could see. "I sense a great bond could form betwixt ye. Strong love."

"Are they speaking to you?" Greer whispered, well aware Ada's pagan spirits did that on occasion. Where most God-fearing folk would shun such, she preferred to respect other people's beliefs. Not only that, but Ada tended to be remarkably accurate.

"Aye." Ada narrowed her eyes on Edmund when he walked two horses out of the stables below. "They are talkin' to me all right."

"He must be leaving for his estate to get the jewels and rally his men." Greer frowned. "I'm surprised he travels alone."

More so that the unsaddled relief horse with him was Teagan's. How curious.

"Given their scheme, I'd imagine yer ma requested that Teagan stay." Ada's gaze lingered on Edmund a moment longer before she headed across the room and rummaged through Greer's trunk. "Besides, the Sassenach is clearly a fighting man. He can hold his own. On the journey back with the jewels, however, 'tis best he have the extra protection."

Ah, how right she'd been about Ada desiring him. Having never seen the particular expression her friend wore, Greer smirked. "You are attracted to him, aren't you?"

"Who?"

"You know full well who." She looked from Edmund to her friend. "He *is* quite handsome."

"He's a bloody Sassenach." Ada pulled out a blue dress and shot Greer an apologetic look. "No offense."

"None taken."

"Stop smiling like that," Ada muttered, urging her to come change.

"Like what?" she asked innocently, rather liking the idea of Ada finding love. Of her children finally having a father.

Ada perked a brow. "Ye know perfectly well, I swore off men."

"I know you said you swore off men."

"Which means I swore off men."

"But she has not sworn off Edmund," Margery chimed in.

"I can tell by the speculative smile on yer face, Margery, and I dinnae see eye to eye on this one." Ada helped Greer into her chemise. "So ye can tell her I will love that Sassenach the day it rains cats and dogs."

"You know that has been known to happen." Greer chuckled as Ada assisted her into her kirtle. "In poorly made structures during heavy rain. It seems animals hide in the rafters only to discover it too wet and flee…or fall."

Ada rolled her eyes and shook her head. "'Twould have to be a verra poorly made structure." Her lips curled up a little when she looked at Greer. "But if it keeps a wee smile on yer face, I guess imagining cats and dogs raining over that Sassenach is all right."

Greer shook her head and kept smiling as Ada helped her with her dress. "You are impossible." She considered her friend. "Why do you think my mother requested that Teagan stay here whilst Edmund retrieves the jewels? Whatever for?"

"So that he might get to know you better." Ada wrapped a belt with a simple chatelaine and chains around Greer's waist. "I get the sense he wants that as well." She met Greer's lingering smile. "Ye should make yer way down to the river again this morn."

"Why?"

"Why do ye think?" Ada gave her a pointed look. "Yer warrior-hero tends to linger there, hoping ye'll happen that way." Her brows shot up. "Which tells me, unlike those before him, he's eager to get to know ye better."

"Or," she countered, "he simply wants to sample what will be his."

"I dinnae think so." Ada shook her head, urged her to sit, and braided her hair. "The lasses say he's different that way."

"What lasses?" She frowned. "And how could they possibly know what way he is in such a short time?"

"Och, ye know better than to ask that." Ada's practiced hands weaved her braid with concise, near-effortless precision. "Servants in this castle know what a lad's like within hours of him being here, never mind spending the whole night. Unlike most, yer warrior-hero has made no advances toward any of them or even eyed them with appreciation." Her gaze went to Greer's face. "That says something."

She tilted Greer's head this way and that, eyeing her handiwork. "And before ye get to wondering where Teagan's tastes might lay, the same applies to the lads as well."

"Mayhap, we simply have a gentleman on our hands," Greer said softly.

"Aye." Ada gave her a knowing look and settled a circlet on her head. "Or a lad who only has eyes for one lass."

Greer thought about that as she went about her morning routine. First prayers at the chapel, then breaking her fast. Could it be a man had come along that wanted her for more than bearing children? More than just her dowry? Well, clearly not in this case because he needed her dowry. That was part of the deal.

Thankfully, she didn't run into anyone in the dining hall or courtyard, but then she was up rather early. Should she make her way to the river? Was Teagan there? If so, should she want to see him? Despite her frustration with the situation as a whole, her heart said yes.

So she headed that way, cutting through the gardens, only to run into her mother.

She should have known better. Mother used to make a habit of sitting out here at sun-up. In fact, at one time, they often did it together. In no mood to speak with her, she tried to backtrack without being seen, but it was too late.

"Good morning, Greer," her mother called out. "I was hoping you might pass this way."

While tempted to keep walking and pretend she didn't hear, she knew better, so turned back and headed her mother's way. She curtsied once she reached her and wished her a good morn.

"I know you would rather not, but 'tis time for us to talk alone at greater length, daughter." Mother started strolling and urged Greer to join her. "'Tis time I explain mine and your father's plan in greater detail so that you have no doubts. So that you know we would *never* shun or abandon you."

Having no choice but to hear her out, Greer fell in step beside her.

"Surely you understand that once Randolph and Isabella's father arranged for me to go to France and Isabella's sister to come here, my brother had no intention of seeing me return." She shook her head. "The exchange, which included Julianna, was done solely so that your uncle would have immunity when France eventually ruled this country."

Greer frowned. "He had such little faith in our fighting men?"

"Whether he did or did not, Randolph is selfish and all about himself." Disgust flashed in her mother's eyes. "He would protect himself on both sides, as would Isabella's father. To that end, I consider them both cowardly traitors." She sighed. "Anyway, as you have likely gleaned by now, the exchange was not just so that I could educate Isabella in English and her sister to teach you French, but so that betrothals could be made."

"Yes," she murmured, having assumed as much. "Uncle would have made a favorable match for Isabella's sister with an English family. In turn, Isabella's father would have done the same when Julianna came of age."

"Correct." Mother's mouth slanted down. "Unfortunately, I fear that might have never happened for our Julianna. Or by the time it did, her virtue would be long gone, and her spirit crushed."

Greer met her frown, alarmed. "What do you mean?"

"I mean, Isabella's father is a dark soul with an eye for young, innocent girls." She stopped walking. Pain flashed in her eyes. "So you see, I had no choice but to get Julianna out of there and leave with Isabella. Not just for Julianna's sake, but Isabella's, too, for her father's eyes turned her way as well." She released a shaky breath. "You have no idea how much I wanted to come back for you first, Greer, but I had nothing to come back with yet. Nothing to barter with."

"Julianna and Isabella are all right, though?" she asked, worried.

How horrifying a situation. "Both are unscathed?"

"Yes." Mother took her hand. "They are both very well. Isabella is pregnant and happily married to Teagan's brother, Malcolm, and Julianna is thriving amongst the MacLauchlins." She cupped Greer's cheek. "You have to know that I always meant to come back for you as did your father, but we had to return with something worthy to exchange. We did not want the kind of life for you and your sister that you have already suffered. So, as I explained last night, we concocted a plan for your father to get the jewels out of here so we could eventually start a new life."

"Why did he not come see me first, though?" Greer asked, suspecting she already knew. "Why not tell me of this plan, so I had hope?"

"If you were already married off, then we were too late," her mother said softly. "There would have been no getting you away from your husband." She shook her head. "My guess is your father very much wanted to say goodbye in person but could not risk those gems being stolen. Was your late husband well-fortified?"

"Yes, very," she confirmed, still unsure how she felt about her father leaving like that. Yet no matter which way she looked at it, she would have preferred her family's safety over her own happiness. "My late husband had a sizeable amount of warriors at his disposal."

"That had to have been it then." Saddened, her mother fingered a tendril of Greer's hair. "I really am so sorry for how things turned out, darling. Sorry that even once we found safe harbor in Scotland, I could not get here sooner. I'm afraid between the weather and needing Edmund to see things through, coming any earlier would have been too risky."

"When did you arrive in Scotland?"

"Around the new year."

"Then, you need not fret." She saw no reason to make her mother suffer. "I only returned a little over a month ago, so coming back any sooner would have been pointless."

"Even so." Her mother held her at shoulder's length, her heart once again in her eyes. "Can you ever forgive me? Can we get past this and start anew? For I have missed you so. Whilst mother and daughter, I like to think we were also friends."

"We were," she whispered, her emotions finally getting the better of her. While she wished her mother had been at least a tad miffed about her having to marry to free her friends, in the end, it *had* been Greer's choice. The only choice as far as she was concerned.

The more important thing right now was knowing she had not been abandoned or forgotten. Moreover, it sounded like her mother was willing to risk everything to get her back. Or, more specifically, willing to give up what might have sustained her and Julianna several lifetimes over.

"'Twill take...time," Greer said softly, her voice wobbly. She preferred forgiveness to bitterness, even if there was little to actually forgive. Her vision blurred with tears. "But yes, I would like to start anew, Mother."

"Oh, thank God." Her mother embraced her and held on tight. "How I have longed to hear those words."

She, at last, embraced her in return and blinked back more tears.

Unfortunately, the sentimental moment didn't last long, though. Not when it was rudely interrupted by the last person she wanted to see.

Chapter Eleven

After waiting by the river in hopes Greer might make her way there, Teagan was just heading back past the gardens when he heard the bite of Bartholomew's voice. He crept close enough to see, then leaned against the wall and strained to listen but caught very little. It appeared the Englishman had just interrupted a tender moment between Cecille and her daughter.

"I have been looking everywhere for you, Greer," it sounded like Bartholomew said, scowling at Cecille. "Did you not receive word I was leaving?"

He smiled, pleased. Things were going as planned. Just so long as Greer didn't join him, that is. Cecille had assured him she would make sure her daughter remained here. Especially considering Bartholomew was leaving due to word of trouble at his estate. Strife to which his future wife should not be subjected.

Even so, Teagan would be relieved once Bartholomew was gone, and Greer remained here.

"He is a *bad* man," wee Besse whispered, appearing out of the shadows. She narrowed her eyes at Bartholomew before joining Teagan against the wall. "Are ye going to rescue Mistress Greer?"

"Aye, but not at this precise moment," he whispered back.

The three in the courtyard continued conversing, the fire in Cecille's eyes telling.

"How come not right now?" Besse asked.

"Because in cases like this," he explained, "'tis best to bide one's time before taking action."

"Ahh." She peeked around the corner at the three of them, then pulled back. "Mistress Greer said ye might do something like that." Her eyes rounded. "So will ye be attacking with a mighty army?"

"Och, there ye are, Besse," her mother exclaimed when she rounded the corner.

Besse put a finger to her lips and pointed into the garden. In turn, her mother shook her head and shooed her daughter along to do chores, then ended up staying. She leaned against the wall, introduced herself as Ada, though he already knew her name, and whispered, "Can ye hear anything, Teagan?"

Somehow he wasn't surprised she already knew his name, too.

"Verra little."

"Hmm." She narrowed her eyes on Bartholomew as he talked. "He is trying to persuade Greer to return to his estate with him. It seems he's been called home due to unrest." She released a dainty snort when she looked at Cecille. "Her mother is having none of it."

He arched his brows at Ada. "Ye can read lips?"

"I can read just about anything." She gave him a telling look before her gaze returned to the others. "Bartholomew doesnae like the idea of leaving Greer behind whilst a wild Scottish beast is in our midst."

"Did he say all that?" Teagan replied, amused.

"Nay, but he might as well have." She gestured that he follow her. "Come, join me for a wee bite. Greer willnae be going anywhere with the likes of that lout."

He frowned, concerned. "How can ye be so sure?"

"Because I have met her mother."

"Verra true," he conceded, following Ada, curious what he might learn from the lass. Like Cecille had discovered, whilst poking around, he'd confirmed she and Greer were fast friends despite her uncle's disapproval. But then Greer was clearly not the type to care about varying stations in life.

Ada tore a piece of freshly baked rye and barley bread in half and handed it to Teagan before urging him to join her for a stroll to the river.

"Us spending time together will get the focus off ye and Greer if ye know what I mean." She winked. "Ye and I being together makes more sense to ignorant minds."

"Aye." No truer words were spoken. He thanked her for the bread. "She takes a big risk being alone with me, aye?"

"Only to her reputation, which I dinnae think she cares about all that much nowadays." She eyed him. "As I'm sure ye know, the bigger risk is to ye in these parts. Now that ye're to be her husband, though, Randolph willnae care as much."

Even though he nodded, he intended to keep an eye out for Greer's uncle. He was not to be trusted.

"How long have ye been here?" he asked Ada.

"Longer than I would like," she replied. "I met Greer several months before she was married off, and it has been over a month since she returned. Altogether, we have known each other for under a year."

"So ye havenae known her long," he replied. "Nor was she married long."

"Nay to both." Ada shook her head. "Greer and I found friendship quickly." She continued eyeing him as they headed down the path. "But then it doesnae take me long to sift out the good from the bad."

"I dinnae imagine it does."

"So are ye truly one of the good ones?" She stopped, planted a fist on her hip, and narrowed her eyes at him. "As ye've likely surmised, I know about yer plan to get my bairns and me out of here."

No "thank ye," for wanting to rescue them, but he imagined she would believe it when she saw it.

"I like to think I'm one of the good ones." Something about Ada's wary gaze prompted him to be honest. "Will I do everything in my power to get ye and yer wee ones out of here? Aye, absolutely. Will I treat Greer well? Most definitely. Will I love her as her good ma hopes? 'Tis impossible to know. Mayhap not."

"Oh, ye'll love her, friend," Ada murmured, her gaze a little haunted as she looked at him. "'Tis impossible for someone capable of love not to." She tilted her head, considering him. "'Tis just a matter of realizing ye are still capable of love. That yer demons can be pacified, and the shadows driven out."

"Can ye see my demons then, lass?" he asked softly, used to dealing with Aunt Mórag. Though most thought her mind snapped from suffering so much loss during the illness, he sometimes wondered if she didn't have a gift. Or mayhap even a curse. Either way, it was *something,* and it was right there in Ada's eyes.

"Aye, I see yer demons." Ada finished her bread. "And they arenae all that different than those plaguing my Greer." Her gaze narrowed a fraction more. "But then I think ye already know that."

"Aye." He finished his bread as well. "And though tempted to ask ye about them, I—"

"Prefer to wait and ask her yerself, aye?"

"Aye."

"Then 'tis her trust ye're after."

"At the verra least."

Ada eyed him for another moment as though seeing straight into his soul before she crouched at the water's edge and splashed water on her face. She hesitated a moment before she glanced over her shoulder at him. "Have ye met Margery yet?"

He shook his head. "Who's Margery?"

"She's the one Greer talks to when ye think she's talking to herself," she said more bluntly than anticipated. When she looked at the water again and went silent, he knew how important his answer was. How much it mattered to her.

"Aye, then I have met her."

"And what do ye make of her?" She stood, crossed her arms over her chest, and eyed him again, gauging his reaction. "What do ye think of a lass that talks to herself so much, then even tends to answer?"

"I think I look forward to getting to know Margery better," he said without hesitation, meaning every word. "As to Greer talking to herself and even answering, it doesnae bother me. Especially if it gives her comfort and a connection, not to mention the escape she so desperately needs."

Ada gestured at the castle. "From all this, aye?"

"Aye," he concurred.

"So ye see her need to escape clearly enough." She cocked her head. "But what's this about a connection?"

"'Tis just as it sounds." He eyed her in return. "And I think ye know that. Though everyone else thinks her mad for talking to someone unseen, my guess is Margery keeps her balanced. A friendly voice in the darkness. A connection not just with hope but mayhap even to the past. Better times." He shrugged. "Often enough during the war, I talked to my brothers or Edmund when they werenae there. 'Twas a way to keep me going."

Ada considered him for a stretch before she finally spoke.

"Well, ye are a rare sort indeed, aren't ye, Teagan MacLauchlin," she murmured. "Undoubtedly broken but at the same time more whole than most."

"I cannae speak to that."

"Of course ye cannae because, in yer own way, ye're as hard on yerself as she is." Ada's gaze narrowed down the path. "Speak of the devil." She shrugged a shoulder. "Or in her case, an angel."

Teagan glanced down the path but saw nothing, nor did he hear anyone coming. "There's no one there."

"Not yet." She urged him to sit beside her on the bench. "But she will be."

He frowned. "Then why would I sit beside ye and give her a false impression?"

Because it surely would.

"There's nothing wrong with sitting beside a new friend." Ada patted the seat. "Now sit. Trust me, this will help things along."

"Help what along?"

"Winning her over before exchanging vows." She sighed and shook her head. "Amongst many things a lass her age should have experienced by now, I dinnae think she's ever felt jealousy. She never cared enough."

He scowled. "'Tis an awful emotion."

"Not a wee bit o' healthy jealousy," she countered. "Right now, Greer sees ye as a man who means to own and lust after her." She perked a brow. "Why not let her see ye as something else? Someone *she* might desire or lust after instead? Give her some of the control?"

"Nay, that isnae what she needs to feel right now." He shook his head. "She needs to feel appreciated for something other than her appearance and what she can provide a man in coin. Not feel more insecure because she came to the wrong conclusion about her friend and future husband."

"Och," Ada whispered, eyeing him with approval before she stood. "Ye'll do just fine, countryman. *Just* fine." This had been a test, and he'd passed. She sauntered back up the path, throwing over her shoulder, "When he gets back, best tell yer Sassenach to stop lusting after me. I dinnae like Englishmen."

"He wouldnae listen to me if I tried," he called after her, unable to help himself. "And he verra much likes wee Scottish lasses."

Foreseeing an entertaining trek north, he chuckled and crouched in front of the water. He noticed Ada hadn't asked more about his plan to get her out, but then he hadn't really expected her to. Folks like her didn't hold out much hope for things. Especially plans like theirs.

As it turned out, Ada was right, and a few moments later, Greer appeared.

Which meant she had crossed her friend on the path.

Relieved to see she hadn't gone with Bartholomew, he stood and nodded hello. "Good morn, lass." He gestured at the bench. "Would ye like to sit?"

"No, thank you." She joined him at the water's edge, her skin a touch drawn. "I just passed Ada."

"Aye, she's verra kind." He hoped she didn't misunderstand things. "She cares a great deal for ye."

"Yes," she said softly. As if chilled, she pulled her thin shawl more securely over her arms. "She's a good friend."

He realized she wasn't jealous in the least but somewhere else in her mind.

"Are ye all right, Greer?" He removed his cloak. "Ye seem cold."

When he went to wrap it around her shoulders, she shifted and lost the grip on her shawl.

"Och," he muttered when he realized what she was trying to hide. Several distinct fingermarks marred the delicate flesh of her upper arm. He frowned at her. "Bartholomew, then?"

He tried to remain calm, so he didn't frighten her. No tightening his jaw. No clenching his fists. Lord, how he longed to wrap his hands around the Englishman's throat so he could squeeze the life out of him.

"'Twas my fault for not joining him in the courtyard when he asked." She thanked him when he put his cloak around her shoulders. "'Tis simple enough to keep him appeased by not inciting…"

When she trailed off, he again asked her if she would like to sit.

"Yes, perhaps I will, after all," she said softly. "Thank you."

"Might I join ye?" he said gently. "Or would ye prefer to be alone for a time?"

"I would rather not be alone if 'tis all the same."

As it happened, she truly surprised him with what she said next.

Chapter Twelve

GREER WASN'T SURE why she said it, but she meant it. She wanted to know Teagan before marrying him. To spend time actually talking to a man and learning who he was. His likes and dislikes. If she were going to be forced into yet another marriage, she wanted to feel more connected than she had with her last husband and certainly more than she did with Bartholomew.

"Aye," Teagan replied. "I would verra much like to meet ye here betwixt now and when we leave and get to know ye better, too, lass."

The tension in her shoulders lessened at his easy response. "Mother said 'twill be a fortnight before Edmund returns with more men."

He nodded. "That's right."

"Do you think 'twill go as smoothly as she hopes?" It seemed so many things could go wrong. "'Tis hard to imagine Bartholomew bowing out gracefully."

He did nothing gracefully, and the proof of that was on her arm. She could only be grateful her mother had managed to keep somewhat calm when Bartholomew yanked her out of the gardens to speak alone. She could tell by the fire in her eyes and the clenching of her hands it had taken a great deal of strength, though.

"It may or may not go smoothly." Teagan nodded with reassurance. "Either way, *'twill* happen, Greer. Edmund and I will get all of ye out of here no matter what it takes."

She glanced at him, curious, sensing something to his passion.

"You have an alternative plan, I take it?"

"Aye, because yer uncle isnae to be trusted." He shook his head. "In fact, we're counting on such."

"I imagine you are," she said slowly, thinking about that. "So, what is this plan?"

"To leave before Edmund returns," he revealed. "If all goes well, he will be awaiting us in the woodland fourteen nights from now."

"'Tis why Edmund took your horse this morn," she murmured. "Because you will be sneaking the lot of us out of here."

"Which makes perfect sense," Margery would have reasoned. "How else would he have done it? In a covered wagon with Ada and the children hiding inside?"

She supposed that wouldn't make sense, would it? For no other reason than her uncle wouldn't spare a wagon for any belongings Greer may want to bring.

"Aye, I couldnae leave my horse behind," Teagan replied. "He's been a comrade-in-arms for far too long."

"Though 'twas risky considering the stable boy could say something," she pointed out, "I understand."

"He willnae say anything," he assured. "Like many here, he isnae a big fan of yer uncle."

"Now that I believe." While tempted to look at him, she kept her eyes averted out of habit, speaking more freely than she meant to. "So, we've a plan, then."

"Aye, I'm sure Cecille meant to tell ye about it before Bartholomew interrupted."

She arched her brows in surprise. "How did you know he interrupted us?"

"Because I was watching ye," he replied more bluntly than she expected. "I was hoping ye might happen this way earlier. When ye didnae, I went in search of ye."

So Ada was right. "You were waiting here for me?"

"Aye." His gaze never left her face. "I want to get to know ye better, too, lass. If that means coming here as often as I can on the chance that ye might be here, I will."

"Oh," she murmured, not sure what to say to that other than it made her happy. "Then 'twas lucky Bartholomew got called away."

"'Twas." His grin told her Edmund might have had something to do with the fortunate timing. "Now, I can only hope the scout we have positioned beyond the castle travels quickly to Edmund, confirming his plan worked so that we might extend Bartholomew's time away."

She rounded her eyes. "Certainly, you do not mean..."

"Nay," he assured when she trailed off, figuring out her presumption easily enough. "Though I admit the idea of ending Bartholomew holds appeal, 'twould be more along the lines of causing *continued* strife at his estate, so he was forced to stay on."

"Ah." Well, that made sense. "It seems you and Edmund thought of everything."

"'Tis habit," he explained, sharing how they had spent ample time together during the war. He also revealed that Edmund wasn't his half-brother but might as well be.

"Then I'm glad Ada and her children have you two helping to free them." Realizing her gaze lingered on his face, she averted her eyes again.

"Ye dinnae need to do that with me, lass," he said gently. "Ye dinnae need to look away."

When she didn't reply, not sure how she should respond, he made things surprisingly clear.

"Though yer dowry is important to helping my clan, please ken that after we marry, if ye wish to go yer own way, I willnae stop ye." He shook his head. "I dinnae want to deny ye love if 'tis what ye seek. I can, however, offer ye friendship, respect, honesty, and protection."

"I do not seek love," she replied, shocked he made such an offer. "I do believe in friendship, though, and would...like that...with you."

She hadn't meant her response to sound so stunted, but in all honesty, she wasn't sure such was possible. Could men and women be friends? Had her mother and father been such? She supposed so.

"Good." When he smiled, her heart skipped a beat. "Then, I look forward to getting to know ye better, Greer."

She met his smile. "And I, you."

"Ye ken what that means, aye?"

Her heart sank. What *did* it mean? What was he going to say? Was this some sort of pre-cursor to lust?

"Just hear the man out before jumping to conclusions," Margery would say. "As it were, I think if he expected something more personal from you, he would be sitting a whole lot closer."

"No, what does it mean?" she asked him, bowing her head.

"First, stop doing that as well." When he tilted her chin up, she pulled back instinctively.

"My apologies." His tone was as gentle as his touch. "I only meant for ye to look me in the eye as yer equal rather than at the ground as if ye're my lesser."

"I..." She searched for the words but simply couldn't find them. So she fell back on what usually worked. "I'm sorry."

"Ye've nothing to be sorry for." Though she got the sense he wanted to sigh, he didn't. "What I meant to say from the start and should have been clear about is that yer days of apologizing for nothing are behind ye. As are yer days of not saying *what* ye want to say *when* ye want to say it."

She looked at him, unsure. "Truly?"

"Truly." He smiled. "How else will I get to know ye? The *real* ye?"

Honestly, she wasn't sure who the *real* her was anymore. The *her* before what had happened years ago. The *her* before her uncle, then her previous husband, and now Bartholomew. She recalled a time when she was more like her mother, but it almost felt like a different life.

"'Twill take time," she murmured.

"Will it, though?" Margery would have said. "With a man like this, I would think it takes little time at all."

"I understand," he replied. "Take all the time ye need. Not just here but as we travel, then at my home. Yer new home."

"In Scotland," she said more to herself than him. It seemed such a foreign concept.

"Now, you are just telling yourself falsehoods." Margery would have rolled her eyes. "At one point in time, we talked about living there. We were going to go on grand adventures, remember?"

She blinked back sudden tears, remembering all too well.

"Are ye all right?" Teagan asked, concerned. "I didnae mean to put so much on ye at once. Truth told, though, there isnae much time left if we hope to get out of England whilst Bartholomew is away."

"No, all's well." She shook her head and stood. "I take no issue with leaving within a fortnight, nor of going to Scotland. I was just…" Though tempted to leave it at that, she found herself telling him the truth. "I just recalled a time when living in Scotland was not such a strange concept."

His brows perked with good reason. "Really?"

"Yes." This time she *did* leave it at that and asked him to join her on the path back to the castle. "Whilst I frequent this spot often, 'tis always best, as a rule, that I do not linger overly long."

Teagan nodded in understanding. "Now that Bartholomew is gone and I am nae being watched so closely, I expect to be here more often until we leave." He glanced her way. "How else will I get to know ye?"

She blushed, looking forward to it despite herself. When was the last time she had looked forward to something?

"It has been far too long," Margery would have said. "And about time."

"So how are we to sneak out of here with Ada and her children when the time comes?" she asked. "One can see a great deal of the surrounding countryside from the castle walls."

"Aye, so we will keep to the forest," he replied, "in the dark of night."

"Ah-ha!" Margery would exclaim. "Be gone riding off into the sunset! 'Twill be a gallant, dangerous hero by night after all."

"What about the jewel?" she asked. "Randolph will pursue us if you don't leave it. In fact, I expect both him and Bartholomew will be after us."

"Aye," he agreed. "Though Edmund will see it delivered to Randolph, we fully expect Randolph and Bartholomew to pursue. Randolph so that he might retrieve his other gems, and Bartholomew out of wounded pride. Therefore, we will be going on a wee bit o' an adventure before we head to MacLauchlin Castle."

"What sort of adventure?" she asked, a little breathless. She envisioned all sorts of exciting things. Stealthy, late-night attacks, then open battle in the bright sunlight. She would wield a blade as she'd long imagined, riding on a steed faster than the wind. Gone would be the time when she cowered to a man. Instead, they would cower before her, shaking and trembling and...

"Greer?" Teagan asked, looking at her curiously.

"Yes, what is it?"

"Nothing, ye just seemed somewhere else for a moment." He smiled. "I do that often, too."

"What?"

"Think more than most," he enlightened. "Anyway, as to this adventure, 'twill keep trouble clear of MacLauchlin Castle. We will join up with and possibly fight alongside enough men to make it clear Randolph and Bartholomew best never seek ye and yers out again."

"Your men, I take it?"

"Mine, Edmund's, and an allied clan who have agreed to help us."

"You understand my uncle and Bartholomew have a substantial amount of warriors, yes?"

"Aye." He grinned. "But, we've got the MacLomains."

"They count many, then?"

"Aye," he confirmed. "And warriors dinnae come much fiercer."

"We can only hope." She shook her head. "Forgive me but—"

"Nay, no more sorry's or forgive me's," he interrupted. "Those arenae words ye need use with me."

When she looked at him, still unsure, he reiterated that he wanted her to speak plainly without fear of consequence. He wanted her to speak her mind.

"I tend to agree with him," Margery would say.

"Me, too," Ada would add.

"No need for your input," she said to her Scottish friend, chuckling. "I will talk to you aloud soon enough."

Teagan merely smiled when she laughed for no reason. Like before, she got the sense he knew she was someplace else in her mind but didn't make her feel crazed for it. Rather, his expression softened as if he knew precisely what she was about. Perhaps even understood.

"Thank you for that," she said impulsively, mortified she had replied to her thoughts aloud. But she meant it. She was grateful for his kindness. For being the only other person besides Ada, and perhaps her own mother, who clearly didn't see her as different.

He looked at her curiously. "Thank ye for what?"

"For helping my friends and me."

"Quick thinking!" Margery would praise. "That makes sense."

"Of course, lass." He steered her around a root in the path. "Is that really what ye meant to say, though?"

How could he possibly suspect that? But then he *did* seem to understand her in ways most didn't. Though it was on the tip of her tongue to say yes, she found herself saying no. More shockingly still, she was truthful. "Whilst, yes, I'm thankful for what you are willing to do for my friends, I'm even more grateful for your kindness when you need not be."

"No need to thank me," he replied. "Especially when I'm the reason ye have to break yer word to Bartholomew, however cruel he may be, and marry a perfect stranger. Ye do have my apologies for that. As to my kindness, 'tis just how 'tis supposed to be."

Was it? She wouldn't know.

She slowed before the woodland path ended. Though it seemed odd to say, she thrilled at saying it. "I will happen this way again in early afternoon."

"I will be here." He kissed the back of her hand; the contact and warmth of his lips startling her. More so, the way his gaze lingered on her face as though seeing her again couldn't come soon enough. As if he genuinely enjoyed her company. Something he confirmed aloud. "And I look forward to it, lass."

As it turned out, he was a man of his word, for he was there later.

Then later that day still.

Then again the next day and the twelve after that, each time more enjoyable than the last. Each one highly anticipated, every moment an absolute pleasure. Exciting and freeing.

It was the thirteenth day, however, that ended up giving her pause.

Chapter Thirteen

Teagan knew the moment he got detained that Greer would wonder what she had done wrong. Though she'd grown more relaxed with him over the past few weeks, she still wasn't as comfortable as he wanted her to be. She struggled with speaking freely and feeling equal.

Yet beneath it all, another woman started to emerge. One with a mind of her own and a passion for life he hadn't expected. Though still somewhat buried, it was there struggling toward the surface. In truth, he'd never been so determined to see anything freed in his life.

Which he would resume trying to do once he pacified Ada.

A man had arrived, who meant to purchase her son. So rather than meeting Greer at the river as promised, he was trying to calm her.

"We cannae wait much longer." Fear flashed in Ada's eyes. "Because he's a man of means, Randolph has convinced him to spend the night, but first thing in the morn, he will be gone with my lad."

"'Twill be all right, lass," he replied, trying to soothe her. Edmund was still at least a day's ride out, assuming all had gone well. "I will see us out of here sooner. Before the morrow. Just let me think, aye?"

"Think?" she exclaimed. "There isnae time to think!"

"Yet, I must just a wee bit longer." He gripped her shoulders and kept her gaze with his. "Lest we act impulsively, and all goes wrong."

"Nay, we cannae have that." She nodded, blinking back tears. "Ye're right. I know it." She shook her head. "That doesnae make this any easier, though."

"I know." He squeezed her shoulders gently. "I'm due to meet Greer. Let me speak to her. See what she thinks."

He'd been watching everything closely and had intended to share his thoughts with everyone later today anyway. Valuing Greer's perspective, he had planned to share it with her first.

"See what she thinks?" Ada asked, almost as though she wasn't sure she heard correctly but grateful she did. "Aye, Greer is thinking better by the moment, isn't she? But then she always did when given half a chance."

"Aye." Once one took the time to get to know Greer and coaxed her out of her shell, she had a remarkably bright mind. But then that was clear in the tales she spun. He'd heard a few of them so far and enjoyed them immensely.

"Someone will let ye know once we've a plan, all right?" he went on.

"Aye." Ada nodded, finally calming. "I will be waiting."

"Ye will, right?" He tilted his head in question. "For we must all do this together."

She nodded again. "I *will* wait."

Content she wouldn't do anything rash, he headed for the river, only to find Greer sitting on the shore with her feet in the water. When she smiled at him over her shoulder, he nearly lost his footing, for she looked so beautiful. Her cheeks were rosy, and she'd removed her coif, so her silky tresses blew in the wind.

"My apologies for the delay." He removed his boots and sat beside her. "How are ye, lass?"

They had visited here a few hours before, but, as always, the time between felt far longer.

"I'm well. Though…"

When she hesitated, he gave her a look. "Dinnae hold back. Ye know better."

They might not have known each other overly long, but she knew how determined he was about this. It wasn't a matter of ordering her like men before him had but wanting her to be herself. Not hold back out of habit.

"Well, if I were to be perfectly honest," she confessed, hesitating before continuing when he arched a brow, "when you were not here ahead of me, I wondered if perhaps you had grown tired of me."

"I dinnae think 'tis possible," he said just as honestly. "Ye are far too interesting."

While most men might have flirted that she was far too beautiful to tire of, which truth told, she was, he found the beauty emerging inside her far more captivating.

"You flatter me," she murmured.

"Aye." And he intended to time and time again. "But 'tis true."

When she eyed him for a moment, hesitant, he smiled and shook his head.

"Dinnae hesitate, lass." He nudged her shoulder with his. "If 'tis on yer mind, then say it. Ask it. Dinnae let it fester."

"If you insist." She sat up a little straighter. "What if I grow uninteresting at some point?"

"Though I dinnae see that happening," he replied with a teasing glint in his eyes, "if it does, we shall talk about it and find a way to make ye more interesting."

She chuckled. "And how does one make someone interesting again?"

"I dinnae know, but it sounds rather interesting in itself, aye?" He chuckled as well and cocked his head. "And what if I grow uninteresting?"

"Then, I suppose the intrigue will only grow to figure out how to make you interesting again, too." Her chuckle dwindled down to a soft smile, her self-confidence improved. "You really are unexpected, Teagan."

"As are ye, Greer." He enjoyed the way her gaze lingered shyly on his face. Enjoyed everything about her, for that matter. Especially the way his name sounded on her lips. How her voice changed a wee bit when she said it. As if she liked voicing it as much as he liked hearing it. He got the impression that wasn't something she was used to with men. That they were so high above her, their names were a privilege to say.

Though he hated to ruin the moment, she would want to know what was going on, so he filled her in on Duncan's plight.

"Oh, dear," she exclaimed.

When she went to stand, he held back from grabbing her wrist to stop her lest the action remind her of Bartholomew.

"There isnae anything we can do at the moment, lass." He gestured at the river. "Please, enjoy the water and let us plan things out, aye? I would like yer thoughts on how we shall get them out of here tonight."

"Tonight?" she exclaimed, sinking back down. "But, of course, tonight." Where days ago, she would have lowered her head and reminded him he was the man so he should decide, now she looked him in the eyes. "What shall we do?"

He shrugged and leaned back on his hands, much preferring to watch her plot. To enjoy her brilliance at work. To see intelligence where others saw madness. "What would *ye* do?"

"I would have to give it some thought." She leaned back on her hands as well and wiggled her toes in the water as if restless to sneak away at once, to start out on their grand adventure straight away. "'Twill have to be very secretive indeed." The way she pondered so briefly told him she'd been mulling this over for some time. Mapping out their '*great* escape' as she would call it when storytelling. "My uncle has men posted everywhere all night."

"He does," Teagan agreed. "Well-armed men at that."

"But are they all seasoned?" she wondered. "I have watched them for a time and am fairly certain they are not."

He slid her a sly look, enjoying this a great deal. "How do ye know?"

"Well, at least one in four prefers drinking ale and eyeing women rather than watching the surrounding countryside."

"Aye," he agreed, impressed. "But what about the three in four? 'Tis a sizeable amount."

"Honestly, and I say this with the utmost respect," she replied, "at least one in three of them are older and, quite frankly, tired and bored." She put a hand to her chest and gazed into the distance as if recalling better times. "As though longing for days of old. Days of excitement and freedom on the battlefield."

"Do ye think being on the battlefield is freedom, then?"

"No, no, quite right." She thought about how to rephrase it. "They long for days of valor and excitement. Days of youth and vigor and..." Greer's eyes rounded, her wee tale taking an unexpected turn. "And perhaps even mysterious activities."

"And what might those be?" he asked, unable to stop a small smile.

"I think we both know." Greer bumped her shoulder against his this time. "Moments in time far more exciting than being in the service of my uncle now. Therefore, they grow bored of late, lost in their own past." She tilted her head, contemplating that. "Which one might think would happen to the other two in four guardsmen, but no."

"Nay?"

"No, most certainly not. They run more ambitious." She shook her head, rueful. "Those are the ones we must sneak past in the end, for they are constantly striving for my uncle's approval."

"Aye," he agreed, yet again impressed. "I came to the same conclusion."

"Did you?"

She looked at him in a way she'd only started doing lately. A confident, passionate way that made him feel different. More alive. Aware of a lass like he'd never been before.

"I *did* come to the same conclusion," he confirmed. "So, what now? With two in four guardsmen paying attention, how should we go about sneaking out of here?"

"'Tis easy." She gestured at the river. "Use this." She slid him a sly grin. "More specifically, use my mother and me."

He narrowed his eyes. "How so?"

"Well, would a squabbling mother and daughter not draw their attention but at the same time be worth leaving alone?" She shrugged. "So whilst mother and I make a show of arguing, you, Ada, and the children head for the river undetected. We will join you soon after." She pointed south. "There's a means to cross over a short way down. From there, a route that passes between watchtowers, then 'tis on to freedom."

"'Tis on to hiding and waiting until Edmund is closer," he corrected, liking the way she thought. "But aye, lass, yers is a sound plan." He nodded with approval. "Ada will be relieved to hear it."

"So, you would not have gone about it any differently?" Greer asked, surprised.

When he shook his head, she eyed him.

"You are not just saying that because of your determination to help me, are you?" She struggled for the right words. "To see the way I think changed?"

"Only when it comes to not speaking yer mind," he replied. "Which ye just did and did so well." He shook his head, absolutely honest, because she deserved nothing less. "Ye came to the same conclusion I did after scouting this land for weeks and watching yer uncle's guardsmen." He winked. "As to ye and yer mother squabbling, that was just pure brilliance."

Though she blushed, her eyes lit up. "You think so?"

"I promised ye the truth in all things, aye?"

"Yes." Her gaze lingered on his face again before she seemed to catch herself and looked at the river once more. "Thank you."

Shockingly enough, she rested her shoulder against his and stayed put this time.

"Nay, thank ye," he murmured, content to leave it at that and simply enjoy the moment. Her. This place in England he would have never thought he'd sit a decade ago. And with an Englishwoman at that.

"I will miss this place," he admitted softly. He knew she grew shy if he admired her too much, so he kept his gaze on the water. "Our time here."

"I will, too," she said just as softly, toying with a pebble beneath the water with her toe. A nervous reaction, he realized. "You have made this place all the more special, and I thank you for that."

He couldn't help but look at her. "The feeling is mutual."

"I'm also hopeful," she whispered. Though she seemed a little surprised she'd said such, she pushed on, her voice a wee bit shaky. "Wishing perhaps…"

"Wishing perhaps what, lass?" he asked when uncertainty flashed in her eyes.

"'Tis nothing," she managed, her attention still on the river. Her cheeks flamed red. "I don't know what I was thinking."

"Yet ye were thinking it," he prompted. "So ye should say it."

"Should I, though?" she wondered. "Is it appropriate?"

"I'm sure 'tis." He couldn't imagine her saying anything inappropriate.

"You may disagree." She finally rallied her courage and looked at him. "Yet, I feel inclined to say it…ask it."

"Then do so," he encouraged, more than curious now. "Because ye dinnae hold back with me, remember?"

"That's right." She swallowed hard. "So, I will just ask you."

As it happened, she did, and it was the very last thing he expected.

Chapter Fourteen

"MIGHT YOU KISS me?" Greer blurted. "Here and now?"

While part of her was shocked she'd asked Teagan such, another part was relieved. Then a third, very insecure part, realized she'd just asked him to do something he might have no interest in doing.

"Of course, if you would rather not," she stammered, "I completely understand for—"

That's all she got out before he tilted her chin and kissed her gently. Tentatively. As though he didn't want to scare her off, which at the moment would be quite impossible. Rather, she'd never wanted a man to stay close more. As close as possible.

Heat curled through her at the feel of his lips against hers. At the way his warm weapon-roughened hand felt when he cupped her cheek. His heat lingered on her lips and skin when he slowly pulled away.

"Thank you," she whispered, unable to find her voice.

"Ye need not thank me, lass," he replied hoarsely. "'Twas my pleasure..." He cleared his throat, his expression a little different. "'Twill always be."

"You must think me horribly forward," she murmured, only to be more forward still. But he made it so easy. "I just...want this to be different."

"As you should," Margery would have said. "And he should know. Hon-

estly, I would hazard to say he would want to."

When Teagan looked at her curiously, she went on, confessing more than she ever dared imagine. But he made it seem so normal. Effortless. As though it were the most natural thing in the world to be so forthright. To share things that weighed on her mind.

"I have never enjoyed the sorts of experiences with men other women have," she explained. "Being admired, pursued, or even kissed." Not to say she hadn't been lusted after by her deceased husband and Bartholomew. It wasn't the same, though. It felt filthy with them. As if she were an object. "So I suppose I hope perhaps this time, despite our union being one of necessity, that I could enjoy at least one of those things. That it would not trouble you overly much."

"*Trouble* me?" Teagan cleared his throat again as though mayhap, as her fanciful mind would have it, still recovering from their kiss. "That is the verra last thing any of those would do." He made her blush again with his bluntness. "Consider yerself verra much admired and, though aye, there is necessity in this, dowry or not, I *would* pursue ye."

"Would you really?" she said softly.

"Aye," he assured without hesitation. "As to the kissing, though I'm surprised ye wanted such, I will kiss ye as often as ye like."

"Why are you surprised?"

"If I were to be perfectly honest, 'tis not something I'd think a pious lass would want before our vows have been exchanged."

Ah, yes. Well, that made sense.

"Whilst devout, I'm not as pious as some might think," she confessed. "Though I visit the chapel daily, and would regardless, before you arrived, 'twas more regularly than usual for the wrong reasons, I'm afraid."

He eyed her for a moment before he seemed to understand. "'Twas a means to avoid Bartholomew, aye?"

"Yes," she confirmed. "And I like to think God was all right with that. As it were, spending time with Him was much preferred."

"No doubt 'twas, and I'm sure God understands." He kept considering her. "Might I be equally frank, lass? About a few things now that we are on topic?"

"I wish you would be."

"Setting aside kissing and my desire to pursue you, 'tis best we marry as soon as possible once we leave," he revealed. "Along those lines, 'tis important ye understand that I dinnae expect consummation. Especially not if ye decide ye dinnae want to stay in the marriage."

That truly did surprise her.

"I figured you would want to marry straight away." She wondered just how blunt she should be. Shockingly enough, she opted for brazen honesty, indeed, saying precisely how she felt. "Whilst I appreciate your offer and still might take you up on it, I'm no longer a blushing bride, Teagan. Therefore, though some might argue otherwise, my virtue need no longer be held to such rigorous standards."

"My goodness, that sounded quite suggestive," Margery would exclaim. "Forget the dark and dangerous escape by night, you have decided you are off on a wicked and sinful adventure!"

It *had* sounded rather bold, hadn't it? But the fact of the matter was, though being a pious widow of status made her chaste in the eyes of the church once more, she was no such thing. Rather, she felt somewhat seasoned. Her elderly husband might not have kissed her, but he lay with her often enough. So yes, no matter how unorthodox, she was no longer a virtuous young girl with high hopes when it came to men.

She was, however, having known Teagan mere days, curious in ways she'd never been before. What would it feel like to have his large, warm hands elsewhere on her body? How might he touch her? Or would he not? Perhaps, like her former husband, he would simply rut with her, expel his seed, then go, leaving nothing but pain betwixt her thighs.

She had never been touched and stroked like she'd heard women whisper about. Certainly never had a man kiss her in the areas of which they spoke. If all that weren't enough, she'd never met a man she wanted to see more of. What did Teagan look like beneath his tunic? Breeches? Her cheeks heated, just envisioning it.

"Whether yer virtue is intact or not," Teagan replied, drawing her attention back to the conversation, "'tis still yer choice, Greer, and I will treat ye accordingly." He issued a devilish little smile. "The kissing, however, could and should happen often, though, aye?"

"It should," she agreed, meeting his smile, glad he'd taken her blunt words in stride. "I would like that."

Though she knew by the way his gaze lingered on her lips, he was tempted to kiss her again right then and there, they returned to chatting, mostly because it came so easily. Talking to him was as effortless as speaking with Ada or Margery. Just as entertaining, too. Therefore, she could safely say men and women *could* be friends because surely such blossomed between them.

In fact, for the first time in years, hours would go by without Margery saying a word. But then, when Greer was with Teagan, there wasn't much time to get a word in edgewise. It was as if they had a great deal of catching up to do. What had her life been like? His? What did they want from their future together or not? And what of children?

"Ye told yer future betrothed all that then?" Ada said later that day, grinning as she helped Greer dress for supper in a fetching green brocade dress. "Ye havenae even spoken to me about that!"

"I know." She smiled softly to herself, recalling Teagan's response to her saying she wanted children. As many as possible. "It seems he does as well."

"'Tis good." Ada set to fashioning Greer's hair once she put a beaded chatelaine around her waist. "Despite, as you say, how much he seemed to surprise himself when he said it." The corner of her mouth curled up. "That he was staring at ye all the while is telling indeed, my friend."

"I can only hope I was not imagining it." She sighed. "We both know my thoughts can get away from me sometimes. That I tend to spin tales and invent things that simply are not there."

"Aye, but not with him, I dinnae think." Ada shook her head and settled a necklace of green gems around Greer's neck. "Based on the way he looks at ye, I dinnae think ye're imagining a thing." Pride lit her eyes. "And to think ye were so bold with him! He must have enjoyed that kiss." She fiddled with a piece of Greer's hair that wouldn't stay in place. "For I highly doubt he would have done it first and risked scaring ye off."

"I think you are probably right." Teagan would not have wanted to upset her by taking something not given freely. She looked at Ada. "So you understand our plan tonight, yes? Where and when you are to meet us?"

"Aye, I ken." She eyed Greer with concern. "Ye realize I willnae be able to bring but a few dresses for ye? Almost none of yer bonnie belongings."

"I understand." She barely glanced at her jewels and trunk full of fineries. "Honestly, most of this does not feel like mine anyway. They were but props to put me on display for uncle's would-be suitors."

"Aye, then." Ada gestured at a dress on the bed. "I've set aside sturdy ankle boots and laid out yer plainest, darkest dress to change into before ye get into a staged squabble with yer ma." She shook her head. "Be sure to wear yer plainest cloak as well. Nothing lined with fur." She held Greer at arm's length, emotional. "Ye've my undying thanks for seeing this through. Might we have a grand adventure together?"

She embraced her friend. "How else can it be?"

Unfortunately, as she soon learned, it could very well be something else entirely.

Chapter Fifteen

OF ALL THE rotten luck.

"That blasted man," Cecille cursed under her breath when Bartholomew arrived just before they sat down to supper. "I had hoped he would not return yet."

"'Tis no matter," Teagan assured softly, grateful he'd been gone this long to begin with. "I will still get ye out of here."

He would, too.

If it were the last thing he did.

In all actuality, considering the swine purchasing Duncan had retired early, Bartholomew's return might not be such a bad thing. Especially if it meant Randolph drank more than usual. If anything, what turned out the more challenging aspect of the Englishman's return was watching him with Greer.

Where he'd envisioned doing dark things to the Sassenach before, now that he knew Greer all that much better, he wanted to draw out Bartholomew's torture for days. Weeks if he could manage it.

"Do not let this rile you, friend," Edmund would say. *"Do not let your demons take over and ruin everything."*

Keeping that in mind, fighting his monsters every step of the way, he clenched his teeth and bore it. Bore the sight of Bartholomew's filthy gaze on sweet Greer. Tolerated the demeaning way in which he talked to her. Tried not to envision the almost healed bruises the man's touch had left on her delicate flesh.

God's truth, it was more than telling by supper's end just how far his feelings for Greer had progressed. How strongly he felt about her. Protective in a way he'd never known before. Not only did he enjoy her company immensely but craved her presence. He wanted to be around her every waking moment. To see her smile and laugh and bloom.

Kissing her today had only amplified the stirrings he already suffered. Stirrings not just of the heart but of the flesh. He couldn't remember a kiss having ever affected him as hers did. A chaste kiss at that, too. But it had. Profoundly. He'd wanted to sample more of her. Slip his tongue into her mouth. Lay her back in the grass. Come between her soft, slender thighs.

When Cecille kicked his leg under the table in warning, he realized with alarm that he'd been staring at Greer. Worse yet, by the lovely warming of her cheeks and the blatant frustration in Bartholomew's regard, his gaze had been telling. How could it not be when he desired her so much? Cared for her?

"When did you say your brother was returning, Scot?" Bartholomew said tightly. "For I imagine you are ready to return to your people."

The way he said "people" made his disgust for them obvious.

"Verra soon," Teagan assured, more concerned by Bartholomew's return the more he thought about it. Would Randolph tell him about the jewel this very night? Before they made their escape?

Because he remained convinced, Cecille's brother would betray them somehow.

"Good," Bartholomew said bluntly about Teagan leaving before his attention turned to Randolph. He went on to complain about miscreants causing problems at his estate hence his delayed return.

"Who were they?" Randolph asked.

"If I only knew." Bartholomew made a dismissive gesture. "Peasants just out to cause trouble, I imagine."

Teagan shared a look with Cecille, who knew all about what Edmund had done. Peasants, his arse. Nay, his friend had received word from their scout and delayed Bartholomew. Something the lout remained clueless about as he rattled on about the worthless poor and their troublesome ways.

Meanwhile, rather than embracing the lively lass she was becoming, or, according to Cecille, who she'd once been, Greer kept her eyes downcast and barely touched her food.

If Teagan were to be perfectly honest, a part of him hoped Bartholomew pursued them to Scotland. He wanted a chance to fight him. To cut him down and make him bleed.

When dining came to an end, he made his way to the corridor Ada was supposed to meet him in, so he knew all was going according to plan. She was there as promised, both eagerness and mayhap a dash of fear in her eyes.

"My bairns are ready to go," she informed.

"Good," he replied. "How do they seem? Are they frightened? Will they be able to do this?"

"Aye, fear naught. Though nervous, they are also excited. More importantly, though, they know how to stick to the shadows and remain unseen."

"They do," he agreed.

"We will sneak down to the river soon," she informed. "Then wait for ye where ye requested." She glanced around to make sure no one was coming. "Cecille and Greer should be arguing in the garden soon."

He nodded, having seen them stroll that way after supper.

"And what are you and your bairns to do if ye get caught?" he asked, going over what they had discussed earlier.

"Say we were but going for a swim." She shrugged. "It wouldnae be the first time I have taken them down there at night."

"And what of the satchels yer carrying?"

"A change of clothes."

He nodded again, satisfied that she had things well in hand. "All right then, stay safe, my friend. I will see ye again soon."

"Aye, ye will."

After they went their separate ways, he made his way down to the courtyard, only for Bartholomew to cut him off.

Reeking of whisky, the Sassenach narrowed his eyes and slurred, "Do you ever sleep, Scotsman? For you always seem to be skulking about in the shadows where you do not belong."

As if he would know despite not being here the past fortnight.

"I'm but out for a wee bit o' fresh air," he replied cordially. It would be so easy to slice his dirk across the man's soft neck. Quickly. Smoothly. Bartholomew would never see it coming.

"I think we both know you have no interest in fresh air," Bartholomew bit out. "Greer is *my* wife, Scot." He shook his head sharply and looked down his nose at Teagan. "Even if she were not, do you honestly think she would ever marry the likes of you?"

"I know she would," he nearly said. "Because she is not your wife."

Fantasy still in play, he would plunge his blade deep into Bartholomew's blackened heart before the Sassenach had a chance to fall to his death.

Though Teagan nearly trembled with repressed rage, somehow, he managed to keep control. Rather, his mind brought him back to the village that awful day. He once again saw the brutalized women. Just like Greer might be at the hands of this man.

That and that alone kept his demons at bay.

His needed to see Greer free of this monster. Free of the life she would suffer with him. So he fought his rage to give her freedom. A chance to be the woman she should be rather than the lass she was becoming with men such as this.

He kept his expression cordial and spoke with a level of calm and respect he by no means felt. "I cannae imagine Mistress Greer ever looking my way. Her honor wouldnae allow it."

"Yet she *did* look your way, did she not?" Bartholomew's eyes narrowed. "Because you lured her somehow, you filthy—"

"Ah, t-t-there you are, Lord Bartholomew," Alfred said, joining them. "I was h-hoping, I might s-speak with you for a m-moment."

"What would I ever have to say to you?" Bartholomew didn't bother looking his way. "You are too simple to hold a decent conversation."

"Quite r-right," Alfred stammered. "'Tis m-my uncle who s-summons you, though. For he has something dire to d-discuss with you."

"Dire, you say?" Bartholomew frowned at him. "Why not speak with me earlier then?"

"I d-do not know." Alfred shook his head. "He awaits you in his c-cabinet chamber."

Bartholomew looked from Alfred to Teagan and back before he muttered under his breath about poor timing and strode off.

"Come on then, simpleton," he snapped over his shoulder, never looking back.

"Y-you must go now," Alfred whispered urgently to Teagan. "You p-proved you were a good man years ago, so t-take Greer and g-g-go as far as you can from this p-place before 'tis too late. Randolph means to betray his s-sister."

Just as they suspected he might.

"Join us," Teagan said without thinking but meaning it. He had no way of knowing where Alfred's allegiances lay as a whole but knew him a man of good conscience. And, because he clearly paid attention, one of stealth and intelligence. "Ye need not stay here with these people."

"And w-where would I g-go?" Alfred shook his head. "Your lot w-would not want me around anymore t-than this one." He gestured in the direction of the river. "Now g-go and keep her s-safe."

"My lot would be happy to have ye," he assured. "And I could use another fighting man to get the lasses and wee bairns out of here safely."

Alfred thought about that before he nodded. "I will try. Until then, 'tis b-best I remain here and l-learn what I can of their p-plans. Perhaps even d-distract them."

He nodded, seeing good sense in that. "Aye, wishing ye the verra best of luck, friend."

"T-to you as well." There was no missing how much Alfred cared for Greer. "Please see her well c-cared for."

He would if it was the last thing he did.

Once Alfred hurried after Bartholomew, Teagan stuck to the shadows and made his way into the woodland behind the estate. He was never more grateful Randolph's castle lacked a moat and second curtain wall. Otherwise, this plan would have been impossible. As it were, the men posted further out tended to scout the land betwixt the watchtowers fairly regularly. At least the two in four he and Greer had discussed.

He caught up with her and the others just over the river, relieved to find everyone well, if not nervous. Though he'd spoken to them about what they needed to do to get out safely, it didn't make the mission any less dangerous.

Fortunately, Cecille and Ada could wield a blade. Though all three of them had given Greer pointers over the past few weeks, it did little to ease his mind. Having watched everyone practice, he knew they weren't ready for what might come at them tonight.

Worse yet, they traveled with bairns.

"Which will very likely make these lasses fight all that much harder," Edmund would say.

As requested, everyone kept quiet and fell in behind him single file. He'd walked these grounds several times over and saw well at night, so made his way without much issue. The key was to watch their step and remain perfectly quiet. Sneezes and coughs must be muffled. No dragging one's feet through dried leaves.

Once they were beyond Randolph's men, he'd get them where they intended to meet Edmund, then pray his friend made it before the Sassenach came looking. Something he feared would happen quickly.

Or, alarmingly enough, far sooner still, based on what happened next.

Chapter Sixteen

When a twig snapped just ahead, and Teagan went still, Greer froze along with the rest of them. Teagan shook his head once, the signal to stay put, and crept forward with his dirk at the ready. The cool night smelled of sweet wildflowers and springtime growth, at odds with the cloying darkness and metallic taste of danger.

"How very exciting!" Margery would whisper. "And granted, a bit frightening." Then she would soothe Greer. "I'm sure Teagan will be just fine, though. He's a seasoned warrior, after all, who, might I add, is in remarkably good shape."

"Now is not the time to admire his physique," she would reply. "For shame!"

"Quite right," Margery would agree. "Though one could argue I'm attempting to put your mind at ease. That no warrior of your uncle's could take down such a magnificent—"

Margery's voice halted when Teagan stopped creeping and sprinted forward. Seconds later, she heard a faint grunt. Her heart leapt into her throat. Was that him? Was he hurt? She was about to go after him, but he reappeared and urged them to follow him once more.

"I think his blade drips with blood," Margery would whisper.

"I think you have a vivid imagination," she replied but wondered at the moisture she swore glistened on the metal. Had he slit a man's throat? Driven him through?

A heartbeat later, Teagan went still again, then whipped his dagger to the left. A strangled sound rang out before a thump resounded nearby.

"Time to move faster," he whispered, moving as quickly as she knew he dared with them following. Her palms grew sweaty. Would one of Randolph's men leap out of nowhere at them? Call for others? If they did, what then?

But she knew. She'd been dreading it all day. Not for herself, but for the others.

If they were caught, not only would it mean severe punishment and inevitable separation for Ada and her children, but Teagan's death. Randolph and Bartholomew would hide it from Edmund, but they would see the Scotsman dead. She knew it without question.

So every step that led them away couldn't come soon enough.

Fast enough.

She wanted them free of this place so that Ada and her children might have a life together. So that she and Teagan might have the same. Though startled at her thoughts, considering so little time had passed since she met him, she truly felt that way. Not only did she feel a blooming friendship with him, but something more.

Something she desperately wanted time to explore.

"You mean love?" Margery would hedge. "That is what we are talking about, yes?"

"Well, I would not go that far," she'd reply. "What do I know of love?"

"Little," Margery would say. "Where you should know far more."

"But we only just met."

"So?"

"So, love takes time."

"How do you know when you know nothing of love?" A silly grin might hover on Margery's face. "I believe love can happen straight away just as easily as it can grow over time."

"Yes," she would reply. "But then you believe in love, to begin with."

"Bloody hell," Teagan cursed under his breath, yanking her from her thoughts seconds before he spun off to the right and engaged a man. A breath later, another warrior came out of nowhere from their left.

Understanding her role until her fighting skills improved, Greer pulled the children close and held her dagger at the ready whilst Ada and her mother dealt with the newcomer.

"'Tis all right," she assured the children, fearing for the others, wishing she could help more. "All will be well."

"You will learn to fight better once you are free of your uncle," Margery assured. "Until then, protecting the little ones is every bit as important."

Greer knew she was right, but that didn't make it any easier.

Teagan side-kicked his opponent to the ground, clamped his hand over his mouth to keep him quiet, then ran a blade across his throat. Meanwhile, Ada kneed the other man in his groin, only for Teagan to close the distance and kill him just as silently as the other.

"Come, now," he said without pause, moving along even faster this time.

Greer's heart beat so hard, she feared that alone might draw attention. Was it too late? Had one of Randolph's men heard his comrade fall? Was he rallying more to arms? Fortunately, despite her burgeoning fears, no cries of alarm rang out, and every step took them farther and farther away until Teagan finally slowed then stopped.

"We are far enough out now that we shouldnae have any more trouble from yer uncle's men at the moment," he whispered. "But, all must remain silent until I say so in case we come upon anyone else out here." He looked from person to person. "Ye ken, aye?"

Everybody nodded, and they were off again.

Though relieved to be beyond her uncle's clutches, she knew Teagan killing those men was unfortunate in more ways than one. Not only would they be discovered, ensuring Teagan's and perhaps even Ada's death, but Greer and Cecille would suffer somehow, too. Had he left them alive, however, they might have roused too quickly and called everyone to arms before they could get away.

The only upside? The spot they were meeting Edmund was relatively unknown in these parts, especially by nobles. The caves they headed for were better known by the poor who, it just so happened, were very good at keeping secrets. But then, according to Edmund, who had informative contacts all over the place, many a fleeing peasant had sought refuge in the well-hidden hideaway over the years.

A spot, as it turned out, they made it to safely without coming across anyone else.

"This is well secluded," her mother mentioned as they made their way down a hidden pathway into a cavernous area beneath a woodland hill. It was so well disguised, all one saw when looking at it was a thick copse of bushes at the base of rocks.

"Aye, 'tis a good place to hide." Because Teagan had an armful of wood he'd gathered, Ada lit a torch they found at the entrance. He gestured deeper into the cave. "There should be a spot to rest just around the bend. According to Edmund, fire cannae be seen from there."

As it happened, there was a small fire pit around the corner and space to rest. Teagan lit a fire, and Greer handed out dried meat, rye bread, and skins of water. Ada and Cecille saw to making the children comfortable beneath thin blankets.

"Might ye spin us some magic, Mistress Greer?" Besse asked on a yawn.

"Of course." She sat on a rock across from them, proud of how well they had done today. "Is there a particular tale you would like to hear?"

"Mayhap, the rest of the one ye started a few weeks ago?"

"Aye," Duncan agreed, glancing from Teagan to Greer. "What happened once yer warrior-hero rode off into the sunset with us?"

"Ye mean the dark of night," Besse corrected.

"Yes, the dark of night," Greer agreed, doing her best to appear whimsical. But then it wasn't that hard once her imagination took over. "Well, after they escaped the dismal fortress with many an exciting battle along the way, they settled into a fairy's nest for the eve."

Besse's eyes widened. "A *fairy's* nest?"

"Is that so safe?" Duncan frowned. "Fairies dinnae know how to wield a blade and protect others."

Besse pouted. "How do ye know?"

"Perhaps they cannot wield a blade," Greer gave the sparks coming off the newborn fire a knowing look, "but they can most certainly control fairy fire."

Duncan cocked his head. "Fairy fire?"

"Oh, *yes*." Greer gestured at the sparks, sure to sound mysterious. "Though we mere mortals only see them dancing around flames in all their dangerous glory, *never* to be touched, fairy fire is wherever fairies go. It protects all the good souls who enter their realm."

"Are *we* good souls?" Besse whispered in awe. Her wide eyes drifted after the sparks.

"The very best," Greer assured. "In fact, children are the most protected of all."

She went on to explain why and continued her story, but Besse and Duncan didn't last long. Soon enough, they were sound asleep. Ada settled beside them, mouthed *thank ye* to Greer, then rested her cheek on Duncan's head, and closed her eyes.

"I'm going to sit by the entrance and keep watch," Teagan said softly.

So soon? She had hoped he might stay a while. Sleep closer.

She must have had a disappointed look on her face because her mother gestured after Teagan once he left. "Why not go sit with him, daughter?" She leaned her head back against the rock and pulled a blanket more securely around her. "I could use the quiet, and I think you could use the conversation."

"Are you sure?" She looked at her mother with concern. "I could sit beside you and keep you warm."

"Oh, I'm plenty warm, darling." She looked from the direction

Teagan went to Greer, blunt to a fault. "Besides, is there not another you would like to keep warm?"

"Mother," she chastised, blushing.

"Well, 'tis true, yes?" Mother replied, sentimental if she were not mistaken. "And 'tis how it should be, Greer. How you should have felt about a man long before now."

"It matters naught at this point," she murmured, considering her mother, glad for the past few weeks together. For the chance to get closer again. "Might I ask you a question?"

"Of course. Anything."

"Were you and Father friends?" She tilted her head, curious. Desperate to know, actually. "And love...you felt it with him, yes? If so, how did you...know?"

"Your father was my closest friend, my dear," her mother said, surprising her. "And yes, we loved one another very much. How did I know, though?" She thought about that. "I suppose there was no singular moment of discovery but a culmination of many. How he treated me, looked at me, made me feel. The respect he afforded me when most men did not." She narrowed her eyes. "I think more than anything, it was how he encouraged me to be myself."

"Strong, then," Greer surmised. "Outspoken against your brother."

"You mean my father," Mother corrected. "My father made him that way." She seemed reflective. "But yes, your father," she seemed to struggle with actually voicing his name, "Phillip knew how difficult it was for me watching my mother cower, so he encouraged me to be different. To see myself as an equal despite my oppressive upbringing."

"You were very lucky to have found him," she replied softly. "'Tis a rare man that encourages such from a woman."

"Not, as you well know now, as rare as one would think." Her gaze again flickered from the direction Teagan went to Greer. "Go be with him, daughter. Go and find your way back to yourself like I once did."

She nodded and was about to head that way when her mother spoke again.

"Just one more thing, darling," she said softly. Her expression grew serious. "Something you must keep in mind."

"What?" she asked.

"There's no time limit on love," her mother said, echoing what Margery would have voiced. "You might not feel it for weeks, months, or even years to come." Wisdom lit her eyes. "Or you might already feel its stirrings without realizing it. For love is that swift sometimes."

Though not as hard to imagine as it once was, she still wasn't sure what she believed. If such was possible. So she nodded politely and finally searched out Teagan, only to find him waiting with a blanket. Moonlight trickled down through the foliage overhead, and white fog curled over the dark forest floor.

She smiled and sat beside him. "You knew I would join you?"

He put the blanket over her. "I had hoped."

"What about you?" She frowned when he didn't wrap up in the blanket, too. "Are you not chilled?"

"Nay." He shook his head. "I'm used to colder weather than this, with less protection."

"Right, because of your years at war," she murmured, glad to be close to him. Resting against him. Breathing in his spicy scent. He'd told her about his time fighting for France, then alongside Scotland's King David II.

"Aye, the war." As tended to happen when he spoke of that time, he sounded adrift. "I dinnae think I've shared so much about it with anyone."

She knew. She could hear it in his voice. "I'm glad you have with me, then. But if it ever becomes too much, you do not have to."

"Nay," he agreed. "I dinnae have to but find myself wanting to." Pain lit his eyes when he looked at her. "I dinnae know why, only that

I do."

Where some women, most in her circles, would find such talk offensive, she did not. If anything, it helped her in some small undefinable way. Perhaps not to face the past, because that felt impossible, but to navigate her way through darker times with someone who understood. Who had seen terrible things and hated every minute of it. A warrior who loathed the evil at the heart of warfare when she thought no such man existed.

Yet for all he shared, she knew he only told but a fraction of it.

War haunted him every bit as much as it did her. He suppressed great pain and grief. Inner demons. They didn't frighten her, though. Rather, they felt kindred. Something he might turn on others during his darkest hour, but never her.

"Well, I'm glad you share with me," she reiterated. "That you speak as freely as you hope I will."

"Aye." His gaze lingered on her face. "As am I, lass. 'Tis...much welcomed."

"Yes," she whispered, suddenly unable to find her voice. Suddenly so aware of him, she could barely breathe. Barely think. "Because I'm here...to listen, that is."

"I know."

When his gaze dropped to her lips, she thought he might kiss her again. Prayed for it, actually. Wanted it so much all of a sudden that when he shook his head and muttered something about staying watchful of his surroundings, she took matters into her own hands.

She wasn't sure why she did it, how she could be so bold, but when Teagan went to turn his face away, she cupped his cheek and kissed him. Though the storyteller in her would say she simply wanted her hero's first kiss on her grand adventure, she knew better.

She wanted the kiss of the broken man he really was underneath.

Though she suspected the two were the same, she wanted the real man, not the made-up hero. The man as flawed and wounded as her.

He didn't pull away from the kiss, but he didn't exactly embrace it either.

Was she being too forward? Bold and brazen? Did he not want this?

Moments later, she got her answer.

Chapter Seventeen

Teagan tried to hold back, he really did, but a man could only be so strong.

"Och, 'tis not a good time, lass," he whispered against Greer's plush lips, grappling with protecting those in his care and the quicksand of her sweet taste. An overwhelming need that, in the end, he was defenseless against. Cupping her cheeks, he tilted his mouth more firmly over hers and finally showed her exactly how a lass should be kissed.

How *she* should be kissed.

Though tentative at first, she blossomed readily enough under the coaxing of his lips and gentle seeking of his tongue. For if he was going to taste her, he would have all of her. The deep recesses of her soft mouth. The play of her tongue against his.

Something she took too far quicker than he anticipated.

So quickly and so well, for that matter, he knew he was in trouble. If he let this go on, his desire might be unstoppable. More than that, he sensed she would open up to him. He could pull her onto him now and lose himself in her heated sheath. Drown in the pleasure and escape she could afford him.

She didn't deserve that, though.

Not here.

Not like this.

And certainly not until they were married.

She may think this a grand adventure, but it was dangerous and her emotions more fragile than she realized. He would not have her look back on her first time with him as a stolen moment without meaning. Nor him as someone who would steal that moment so callously.

"We cannae," he whispered, breaking off the kiss before it was too late, and he couldn't stop himself. He rested his forehead against hers. "Not here. 'Tis far too dangerous."

"I'm sorry, I—"

"Nay." He pressed a finger to her kiss-swollen lips. "No being sorry. Especially not for this…never for this."

Needing her to understand, he looked at her and remained truthful. It wasn't all about his inability to protect everyone if he lost himself in lust.

"With or without yer virtue, and pious or not, if I keep kissing ye 'twill soon become impossible to stop," he confessed. "And I willnae lay with ye the first time unwed out in the middle of nowhere on the cold, hard ground." He was more honest still. "When I take ye, and I will if ye'll have me, 'twill be on a proper bed after the wooing ye deserve."

Her lips curled up. "Wooing?"

He met her smile, caught yet again by how easily it came. How he liked the feel of it once more. Especially when it was for her. "Aye, *wooing*."

Something better done once honesty lay betwixt them. He should tell her that he'd lied to get her away from Randolph and Bartholomew. That he would have saved her friends whether or not she agreed to marry him.

Yet, he hesitated, not wanting to ruin the lighthearted moment.

"Was what I enjoyed the past few weeks not wooing?" A soft smile lingered on her face. "The long conversations? Laughter? Your kindness? Even, I dare say, your flirtation?"

"Aye," he acknowledged. "But 'twas only a few weeks' worth. Ye deserve more than that."

Just as soon as he told her the truth. What sort of man would he be if he didn't? In all honesty, what did it say about him that he hadn't already?

"That you are the kind of man who puts getting innocent lasses away from monsters before all else," Edmund would say.

"I cannot speak to what I do and do not deserve," she said softly. "I can say, however, that I've enjoyed our time together thus far and look forward to what lies ahead." She surprised him with her forthrightness. "That said, whilst wooing is always appreciated, I'm of the mind 'tis not necessary nor prudent to experiencing…more."

He might have seen many things coming, but not that.

Not that she was eager to make love.

The fact that she'd never been kissed before and lost her virtue to an old man was unfortunate. In truth, he was somewhat shocked she wasn't turned off to the act altogether after that. But then there was a fire in Greer. Passion struggling to break free. A lass who, by the grace of God, had not yet been crushed by monsters.

Day by day, she reminded him more of her mother with her straightforward talk, and he liked it immensely. Not just because she grew more comfortable with him, but because he genuinely liked how she saw things. How she said things.

In turn, he found himself saying how he felt, too.

"We will take things as they come." He trailed his finger along her jaw. "As to wooing, it comes in many forms." He traced the pad of his thumb over her lower lip, eager for the moment he could explore the rest of her body. For when he could show her how bonnie a lass could feel simply by the way a man touched and looked at her. How wooing and seduction could cross over so very easily. "Soon, lass. When 'tis right, aye?"

"Yes," she whispered. "When 'tis right."

Before he grew too fixated on her lips again, he wrapped his arm around her shoulders, tucked her against his side, and rested his dagger on his lap.

"You won't sleep, will you?" she said softly. "Like you rarely did during the war when watching for the enemy?"

"Nay," he replied. "I willnae sleep, but ye will." He tucked the blanket more firmly around her. "Sleep, so ye are rested for when Edmund comes, and ye truly begin yer grand adventure, aye?"

"Yes," she murmured on a yawn. "Though 'twould be better if I kept you company, would it not?"

"Nay, 'tis best I remain vigilant." He kissed the top of her head when she cozied down against him. "And I dinnae think so clearly when ye speak."

Or do much of anything, really. Everything about her was distracting. Overly alluring.

"'Tis good to know I'm still interesting," she whispered.

"Oh, ye are," he assured. "More so than most."

"I don't know about that," she whispered drowsily. "I once knew someone more interesting. You would have liked her as much as she likes you, I think."

Something about the sad tone in her voice caught his attention.

"I'm sure I would." He rested his hand over hers. "Ye must miss her verra much."

"You have no idea," she whispered so softly he almost didn't catch it. "Though the pain *has* lessened some these past few weeks. I think I have you to thank for that, too."

While tempted to ask her more, to understand the sadness in her voice, he did not. He wouldn't take advantage of her exhausted state but wait until she shared more later if she were so inclined.

As it happened, he spent every waking moment that night thinking about her. Of what he hoped lay ahead for them. First off, teaching her how to fight. He knew how frustrated she was that she knew so little. She wanted to learn how to wield a blade better. To defend herself and others if need be.

While part of him rebelled at the idea of her being anywhere near battling, he found her ambitions admirable. Her need to become more of a protector than she already was. For she was very much one when it came to those she cared about. So said her every action around Ada and her wee bairns.

Though his eyes remained open, he never had a more restful eve than he did with Greer tucked against his side. Every so often, she murmured to Margery but inevitably cuddled closer to him, breathed deeply, and drifted back off.

"Ah, but a mother could not ask for a more heartwarming scene upon waking," Cecille said softly when she appeared in the wee hours of the morn. Her knowing gaze went from Teagan to her slumbering daughter. A small, teasing smile ghosted her face. "Nice to see you continuing to merely 'like' her."

Rather than move and risk waking Greer, he quirked the corner of his mouth, may she make of it what she would. Naturally, she took that as an invitation to go on.

"You make a lovely couple, just as I knew you would." Her smile wavered as she looked at Greer, her gaze suddenly different. Mayhap a tad haunted. "Truly a perfect fit for one another."

Without a doubt, whatever Greer had experienced put that look there. A look that saw the demons plaguing her daughter's past. Demons with sharper teeth than those of the pompous, ignorant men who'd been in her life since.

On several occasions, he'd been tempted to ask Greer what happened in the hallway the first eve he'd arrived at the castle. When she thought herself alone and spoke with such angst to who he now knew was Margery.

Though inclined to comfort her, he knew better. Even if Bartholomew hadn't interrupted, she wasn't ready. Not yet. When she was, she would tell him. Whatever it was, the voice in her head walked hand and hand with her demons. For he'd never seen such torture on a lass's face. Torture he recognized because he carried the same.

Self-blame and self-loathing.

"Good morn," Greer murmured, pulling him from his thoughts. She blinked against the dim morning light before she realized her mother was there as well. "To you both."

"Good morn, daughter." Cecille smiled softly. "How do you fare?"

"Well, thank you," Greer said on a yawn. "But then I was quite comfortable."

When she looked at him sleepily, her eyes half-mast and dewy, he swore his heart skipped a beat. More than that, he realized just how much he wanted to see such every morning. Her against him, warm and safe in his arms. Not only that, but beautiful in every sense of the word. A type of beauty he knew would never fade, no matter her age.

"Oh, yes," Cecille murmured. Her astute gaze never left them. "Very comfortable indeed, I imagine."

Though she never elaborated, he knew Cecille saw what he felt.

The first stirrings of love.

In truth, he suspected he'd felt them far sooner, if not the moment he laid eyes on Greer when she protected Duncan at the castle. But when she awoke that morning in his arms, and her gaze turned to his face first thing, he began to get a sense of something much deeper. Something that finally made him understand what he saw between his brothers and their lasses.

Was such possible, though? Or was it too soon? Where Keenan and Fionna had known one another for years, Malcolm and Isabella found love rather quickly. Genuine love at that. Love seen plain as day when they looked at one another.

"So do ye think we will see yer Sassenach today?" Ada said, appearing at the entrance of the cave. She stretched and grinned when Greer finally pulled away. "Och, dinnae move on my account."

He agreed because his arms felt too empty when Greer wasn't in them. A sensation he'd never experienced with a lass. A sensation he didn't much like.

"Unless something detains him, Edmund should arrive today," he replied to Ada. "Until then, we wait right here. 'Tis too risky to do otherwise."

She nodded and eyed the area. "Is there water to be had? My bairns will need some."

"Aye." He nodded. "Bring me yer skins, and I will see them filled."

He would see to food, too, be it whatever he could find in the immediate vicinity.

As it turned out, the day proved blissfully uneventful, their fare that of river water and hare meat. Nevertheless, none came upon them, and the day wore on.

Though he worried how he would care for everyone if Edmund didn't show up, time still passed pleasurably. How else could it be with Greer and her inquisitive mind? With the *real* her surfacing even more now that she was free of her uncle's estate? He taught her how to lay a trap and skin an animal, which though she turned a wee bit green, she followed readily enough.

"It gets easier each time," Duncan assured, giving pointers to Teagan all the while. "Ye'll see."

"Should she have to, though?" Besse scrunched her nose. "For Mistress Greer is a true lady."

"And true ladies should know how to take care of themselves," Greer counseled, flinching when Teagan showed her how to spear the hare on a spit and put it over the fire.

Besse sighed. "If ye say so."

"I do." Greer nodded at Teagan with reassurance when he wondered if mayhap her stomach was going to upturn altogether.

She was about to say more to Besse when he sensed something and put a finger to his lips. He gestured that everyone stayed put, unsheathed his blade slowly, and made his way toward the entrance of the cave. God above, let it be Edmund and not Randolph or Bartholomew. Let him get these lasses and bairns out of here safely.

Would it be his friend?

Or would it be his enemies?

Half a breath later, he found out.

Chapter Eighteen

GREER COULD SAY without hesitation that the more she got to know Teagan, the more she loathed him putting himself at the head of all incoming danger.

"Blast it, I need to learn to wield this better," she cursed, clutching her dagger as they awaited word from Teagan, who'd just crept toward the front of the cave.

"Me, too," Besse whispered in agreement. "At least yer ma doesnae say nay, ye're too young."

"Shh," Ada hissed, watchful, her gaze glued to the cave entrance. She kept a hand hovered just over Besse's mouth lest she speak again.

Greer barely breathed. Was this it? Had they come all this way only to be stopped at the threshold of true escape? Seized at the onset of their grand adventure?

Even as she feared for their lives, her mind wandered to what that kiss last night had felt like.

"'Twas wonderful, was it not?" Margery would have whispered, keeping Greer's mind on the kiss, rather than the stark fear she felt watching Teagan await a possible enemy. Perhaps even impending death. "I told you years ago that someday we would kiss a man like that. We would feel what you felt. And just look, you did, so I was right!"

Yes, she was.

More than she could ever know.

There weren't enough words in any storyteller's arsenal to describe it either. To convey how all-encompassing his kiss had felt.

Intimate and loving. Passionate and lustful. When his tongue slipped into her mouth, a myriad of sensations coursed through her body. A heaviness in her breasts. An aching throb betwixt her thighs.

"'Tis all right," Teagan called back, interrupting her thoughts. "'Tis Edmund."

"Oh, thank Goodness," Cecille exclaimed, breathing a sigh of relief.

"Aye," Ada agreed. She kissed the top of Besse's head before she pulled her children close. "Though I never thought I'd say it of the Sassenach, praise God indeed."

"Aye, lassie, and ye best not forget it," Edmund called out, evidently hearing as well as Teagan.

Besse scratched her head. "The Sassenach sounds just like us."

"Aye." Ada rolled her eyes. "'Tis offending, to say the least."

Yet Greer didn't miss the twinkle of interest in her friend's eyes when Teagan and Edmund ducked into the cave and joined them.

"'Tis good to see you again, friend." Cecille smiled at Edmund. "So very good."

He nodded graciously at Cecille and winked at Ada. "Where else would I be?"

"Dining with yer fellow Sassenach." Ada muttered a vague thanks under her breath before peering out the cave entrance. "Have ye men with ye then?"

"Aye, lass." He clearly looked forward to goading Ada every step of the way. "Like myself, a mixed lot. A wee bit o' Scots and an Englishman or two."

"A mixed breed, then?" Duncan got out before Ada put him in his place.

"Dinnae talk like that, lad," she scolded. "Count him blessed to be Scottish and do what ye can to help him grapple with his Sassenach blood."

"Bloody hell, but ye're a sharp-tongued lass." Not offended in the least, Edmund smiled broadly, switching effortlessly to sounding English. "Might we travel then? Off to the wilds of Scotland and more sharp-tongued women like you?"

"Oh, I dinnae think ye'll find lasses quite like my good ma," Besse began before Ada shooed her along, scowling at Edmund in passing despite him being her savior.

"Ah, but 'twas worth all this for that wee lass alone." Edmund admired Ada's backside before his smile fell, and he turned his attention to Teagan, Greer, and Cecille. "What happened? Based on Randolph and Bartholomew's men already scouring about, I assume things did not go as planned."

"Nay." Teagan shook his head and filled him in. "We must leave straight away and get over the border as soon as possible."

"Aye, you did what you must, and I agree with your decision." Edmund shook his head. "This does not change our plans any. I will still say I caught word of your betrayal and pursued you."

"Whilst I appreciate yer help, ye need not go further than the border." Teagan doused the fire, and they headed outside. "Ye could just as easily head home, lest risk yer good name."

"And leave you to get these women and children to their final destination alone?" Edmund shot him a look that he should know better than to suggest it. "'Twill not happen, friend. 'Tis equally dangerous territory north of the border." He shrugged as they joined the others. "Besides, you know I'm not much worried about my good name."

Ada gestured in the direction of Randolph's castle and eyed Edmund. "So what happens when that lot catches up with us? I'd think more than just yer good name would be at stake." Her eyes narrowed. "Unless ye take us prisoner and hand us over."

"That willnae happen."

"Then *'tis* truly yer good name on the line."

"'Tis nothing for you to worry yourself over, lovely."

"Dinnae confuse worry with simple curiosity, Sassenach," she replied a bit too quickly. She glanced at the Englishmen he had with him. "So, if I am nae mistaken, ye might have verra well sentenced these lads to certain death."

"We understand the risks," one of the men replied. He issued a loyal nod to Edmund. "And we came willingly."

"Aye?" Ada's gaze narrowed on the man. "Whilst ye've my deepest thanks, ye ken ye're riding into hostile territory? 'Tis dangerous up that way, especially for a Sassenach."

"They ride to the border and no further," Edmund clarified. "From there, they will go in a different direction in hopes of confusing our potential pursuers."

"A move just as risky." Ada eyed the men dubiously. "And surprising."

"As you well know, having met Greer and her mother, not all English are your enemy, lass." Edmund glanced from her children back to her. "Far more than you think would not approve of Randolph owning Scots and their wee bairns, never mind splitting them apart."

Though Ada only offered a non-committal grunt in reply, she seemed less wary.

Edmund looked at Cecille. "The gem has been delivered to your brother, but I doubt 'twill be enough."

"With men like Randolph, 'tis never enough." Teagan shook his head. "Betwixt his wounded pride that his Scots got away and the jewels I'm sure he suspects Cecille still has, 'twill be surprising if he doesnae pursue ye straight into Scotland."

Cecille sighed and nodded in agreement, her concerned gaze on Edmund. "What did Randolph say when the gem was delivered?" Her brows tugged together. "Assuming, of course, he allowed your messenger to leave."

"He did, but then he was in quite the stir over receiving the gem," Edmund replied. "I think he was less concerned, at the moment, about his niece or escaped Scots. Rather, his mind was on what that jewel could do for him."

She shook her head. "Which, naturally, did not last long."

"No," he agreed. "Which is why we must leave soon."

"What of Bartholomew?" Worry lit Ada's eyes when she looked at Greer. "Mark my words, as long as he's still breathing, that man willnae let ye go."

"Then may God bring his neck to my blade sooner rather than later," Teagan muttered.

Having a bad feeling about this, Greer frowned.

Moreover, she understood why he might not want such a thing to happen.

Chapter Nineteen

"Truly, I hear Bartholomew's very good with a sword," Greer insisted, not for the first time later that eve. She shook her head. "You would not know it looking at him, but that is what people say."

They had been riding at a good pace and were closing in on the border. He and Greer rode together, Edmund with Duncan and Ada with Besse. Thankfully, the moon was full enough that they didn't need to light torches.

"I'm better with a sword, lass," Teagan reassured yet again. Whether he was or wasn't, he was touched by her concern over his welfare and didn't want her to worry. "So dinnae fret, aye?"

"I'm afraid such is impossible." She glanced over her shoulder at him. "I fear breaking my word to Bartholomew will be your ruin."

About that.

Enough with lies betwixt them.

This seemed as good an opening as any to come clean. He would not marry Greer without her knowing the truth.

"If for some reason Bartholomew *was* my ruin 'twould not be yer fault." He shook his head. "Nay, I would have no one to blame but myself."

When she glanced at him in confusion, he went on.

"I would have gotten Ada and her bairns away from Randolph whether or not ye agreed to be my wife." Teagan sighed. "I only gave ye an ultimatum because I couldnae stand the thought of ye with Bartholomew." He prayed she understood. "Whilst I'm sorry I lied, I wouldnae have ye suffer a life with him. Because *'twould* have been suffering."

Other than the slight flare of her pupils, it was impossible to gauge her response. Rather than reply right away, she faced forward, evidently coming to terms with his revelation. When her response eventually did come, it wasn't quite what he expected but should have anticipated.

"Thank you for your honesty," she replied. "In return, I will give you equal honesty." She looked over her shoulder again. "Though I'm not fond of breaking my word, I like to think God would understand. That He would have wanted me free of a man like Bartholomew." Her lips curled down. "What bothers me more is you marrying me for my dowry."

She sighed and faced forward again, continuing before he could respond. "I understand 'tis how things are done, but that does not change the fact I wish it were otherwise. Whilst we have spoken at length about your clan's hardship, and I'm eager to assist, I cannot help but wish it were of my own volition. That I was wanted for more than what I bring in coin."

"I ken." And he did. In its own way, it made her no different than what Ada and her bairns suffered at the hands of Randolph. They were no more than commodities. "Ye dinnae know how much I wish things were different. That we could have met under less dire circumstances."

Never more serious, he tilted her chin until she looked at him again. "Dowry or not, I would have much preferred ye picking me rather than the other way around. There's a..." He struggled to find the words to convey his confusion as of late. "There's something disconcerting in knowing ye're not marrying me by choice. That ye didnae choose me nor necessarily want me, but that I was thrust upon ye. 'Twould make me much happier to think ye were here because there was no place else ye'd rather be."

Her eyes dampened at his admission. "Do you really feel that way?"

"Aye." He kept with truth, however foreign the words. "I dinnae know much about love, but I *do* know I enjoy yer company a great deal and want ye by my side, coin or no coin."

He did, too. In fact, if her dowry was stolen away at this very moment, he would still want her as his wife, the pact he'd made with his brothers, be damned. He would find another way to raise coin for his clan. Just so long as she was by his side, he would figure things out.

Clearly trying to rally her emotions, Greer offered a jerky nod and looked forward again.

He hoped he'd conveyed himself well. That she understood what he meant. How serious he was. Sharing his feelings wasn't something he did, so he had nothing to fall back on. He made to say more, to make himself clearer if need be, but the man Edmund had sent ahead to scout returned.

"There are men in waiting just around the bend," he reported.

Could it be his brothers? Edmund had sent word to them when they first concocted their plan to get Ada and her children away from Randolph.

"Friend or foe?" Edmund asked.

"I don't know." His man shook his head. "All I know is there are far too many for us to pass safely into Scotland if they are the enemy."

"Then we must find out." Edmund withdrew his sword when numerous shadows appeared through the woodland ahead. "And 'twill be sooner rather than later by the looks of it."

Chapter Twenty

"Stand down," Teagan said to Edmund and his men when everyone unsheathed their blades. "They are friends." He swung off his horse, grinning as he clasped hands with the two men who stepped out of the woodland. "Adlin and Tiernan, good to see ye, my friends!"

Greer sighed in relief when Teagan introduced them to everyone. They were the MacLomains he'd spoken about. Both tall and handsome, clearly father and son, one appeared to be around her mother's age, the other Teagan's.

Adlin grinned at Teagan. "Good to see ye as well, lad." He nodded hello to the rest of them. "All of ye, for that matter." He swung back onto his horse. "Ye were close to the border, so we thought ye could use an escort."

"Aye, 'tis appreciated." Teagan swung back onto his horse as well. "We've a scout behind us, but havenae heard anything, so I dinnae think we are in immediate danger."

"Nay," Tiernan agreed, mounting his horse. "Our scout reports them heading in this direction but still a way out. If anything, they should arrive on the morn."

"Ye didnae need to put one of yer men at such risk." Teagan shook his head. "But ye've our thanks, to be sure."

"We are allies, are we not?" Adlin gestured that they follow. "Besides, 'twas not one of our men but yers."

"Och," Teagan muttered, figuring it out in no time. "Malcolm, then?"

"Aye, he claimed only the best tracker would see to his brother." Adlin chuckled. "That being him, of course." He nodded with approval. "I tend to agree, considering the distance he covered so quickly, undetected." He shrugged. "Though I'll admit I was surprised he didnae join ye."

"Now what fun is there in that?" a swarthy, handsome Scotsman asked, grinning as he appeared on horseback out of the woodland. He clasped hands with Teagan. "Good to see ye, brother."

"Aye." He met his brother's grin and introduced him to Ada, the children, and Greer. "With any luck, Greer and I will be married this eve."

"'Tis nice to finally meet ye, lass." Malcolm glanced from her to Teagan, smiling all the wider. "I see ye've already brought me home a much-changed brother."

Had she really? She glanced over her shoulder at Teagan, who smiled in return. That must be what Malcolm referred to, for he *did* seem happier as a whole, didn't he? Though shadows still haunted his eyes, they were not as fierce as they'd been that first day in the courtyard.

"Changed indeed," Malcolm echoed.

"But of course." Her mother met Malcolm's smile. "Did I not say such might happen?"

She had? Greer wondered what she'd said specifically.

"The specifics do not matter," Margery would say. "I imagine the gist of it was that you would be his perfect match."

Quite honestly, she thrilled at the thought. That they might, despite being an arranged marriage, be that well suited to one another.

What Teagan had said about wishing she'd chosen him to be her husband had meant a great deal. He'd seemed so genuine. Even a touch sad. As though the idea of her wanting him seemed out of reach somehow. That perhaps he wasn't worthy enough. But then he *had* seemed upset about lying to her. He hadn't liked giving her a false ultimatum to free her friends from Randolph.

"'Twas downright heroic in my opinion," Margery would mutter. "And don't bother arguing it because you never gave your word to Bartholomew to begin with. He was a monster and only bound to become more of one." She'd narrow her eyes, not letting Greer get a word in edgewise. "Setting all that aside, I would think you grateful, for your future husband values honesty above all things. He did not have to tell you the truth. Yet he did because he wants to earn your trust. To have no lies betwixt you before starting your life together."

Life together? When another thrill shot through her, she realized just how much she hoped that would happen. That they would be free of Bartholomew and Randolph and able to start a life she never thought possible. One full of friendship and kindness instead of loneliness and cruelty. Because it *would* be that way with Teagan. She had no doubt.

"Come along, then," Adlin said, interrupting her thoughts. "There is room enough for all at a tavern just over the border. We can make a good stance from there on the morn."

"'Twill be more than a stance." Duncan's eyes widened on the big MacLomain warriors falling in around them. "The bloody Sassenach willnae step one foot in Scotland with the likes of ye at its gate!"

"Watch yer language," Ada muttered, nodding thanks to Adlin and Tiernan. "Though he makes a good point."

"Aye, 'twill be a good showing," Adlin acknowledged, yet Greer sensed more to it. As did Teagan, it seemed.

"What did ye see back there, Malcolm?" Teagan asked, suspecting it had to do with who followed. "How many do they count?"

"More than ye'd probably like," Malcolm replied. "Enough for a good battle on the morn." He winked at Duncan. "But not nearly enough to defeat us."

After Edmund bid farewell to his men, Adlin and Tiernan pulled out ahead, and Edmund fell in beside Ada. Malcolm fell back with the rest of them for privacy, so they didn't worry the children.

"Randolph is amassing quite a few fighting men," Malcolm revealed. "From what I could tell, so many that 'twill leave little protection behind at his holding."

"Damn him," her mother cursed before apologizing for her language. "Never was there a more selfish, prideful, greedy man than my brother."

"What of Bartholomew?" Teagan asked Malcolm. "Ye were given a description of him too, aye?"

"Aye, he is coming." He gave Teagan a look. "He sent a man off, as well. A messenger, I would say."

"So he rallies more men from his estate," Teagan surmised.

Malcolm nodded. "That would be my guess."

Greer heard the concern in Teagan's voice. "What of Keenan? Tell me he isnae here but back protecting our people just in case." He sighed. "'Twould not be all that hard for Randolph to learn the location of our clan."

"No," her mother agreed, equally concerned. "Yet, as you know, I'm hoping he assumes I kept the remainder of the jewels on my person rather than risk leaving them at the castle. Hence, he will pursue me. Not just that, but I'm sure he wants to retrieve Greer, Ada, and the children as he considers them his property."

"Bloody bastard." Malcolm glanced Teagan's way. "Aye, though he wasnae happy about it, Keenan stayed behind, as did half our fighting men."

"Good," Teagan replied. "Hopefully, 'twill matter naught in the end, and all will go as planned anyway."

After that, little was said until they were safely over the border and the risk of being overheard lessened.

"Welcome to Scotland," Teagan murmured in her ear. "May ye someday love it as I do."

Though the woodland had changed little, in some strange way, it felt like everything transformed regardless. That the real adventure had only just begun.

"That's because it has," Margery would exclaim. "Oh, but the times we would have had here! Times you will still have to tell me all about."

Greer blinked back tears when emotion overwhelmed her. *"As if you will not be with me every step of the way."*

"Perhaps," Margery replied softly, seeming closer yet further away, all at once. "But mayhap not always. Not now that you have made a friend of Teagan and will make many more friends to keep you company."

"Are you all right, lass?" Teagan said softly, wrapping his arm a bit more firmly around her waist in comfort.

"I am," she whispered. "Or at least I will be."

"Ye will," he reassured her, *almost* as if he understood what she meant. That her words had nothing to do with the men pursuing them.

"I think he does understand on some level," Margery would say. "He's a good man, my friend. He deserves you as much as you deserve him. You realize that, yes?"

"Yes," she would reply because she did realize such. She felt it soul-deep.

"Then why not let him know?" Margery would say. "Why not give him the new beginning he gives you? Why not give him what you know he longs for? Because his were not hollow, meaningless words earlier. They were said from a heart as damaged as yours." Her friend would likely pause, giving her a moment to think about it. "Unless, of course, you do not feel the same way about him that he feels about you?"

"You know full well how I feel," she murmured, frowning when she realized she'd spoken aloud.

"Aye, it has not been easy for ye," Teagan said softly. "But hopefully, things will get better."

Yet again, she sensed he knew she'd been talking to herself but didn't call her out.

This time, however, more needed to be said because Margery was right.

"Things *will* get better," she agreed, convinced of it. "But only if we begin this as we should."

That in mind, coming to a swift decision, she looked over her shoulder and said the last thing he probably expected.

Chapter Twenty-One

"WILL YOU MARRY me, Teagan MacLauchlin?"

Teagan was positive he would remember that moment for the rest of his days. The nervousness and hope in Greer's beautiful gaze when she looked him dead in the eye and asked him to marry her. Though yes, she'd done it as a kindness, he could see clearly that she genuinely wanted to as well.

She was choosing *him*.

Naturally, he'd said 'aye' without hesitation, truly never so happy.

Or mayhap that wasn't true.

Because when she came down the tavern stairs later that eve with Cecille and Ada, he was happier still. Despite having two Englishwomen among them, the townsfolk were welcoming, even providing barrels of cold water in their rooms for bathing. More than that, their holy man was willing to marry "a Scot and a *Sassenach*?" as he'd put it with wide-eyes.

But agree he did, now here Greer was, easily the most beautiful lass in the room. Likely the whole of Scotland. She wore a simple blue woolen dress that highlighted her shimmering eyes and a ring of flowers around her head. Her cheeks were rosy, and her hair soft and flowing.

"Ye look verra bonnie, lass," he complimented her hoarsely, his voice not working quite right.

"Yes, she does," Cecille murmured, tears in her eyes as she looked at her daughter.

"Aye, she has a special shine about her tonight, to be sure." Ada fiddled with Greer's headpiece, trying to hide her own damp eyes.

"Ye're a lucky man," Adlin said to Teagan before telling Greer how beautiful she looked, as did everyone else.

"Thank you." She smiled softly at them. "You are too kind."

"But truthful," Teagan replied, eager to make her his wife. "Though the chapel isnae much to look at, the holy man awaits us there."

"A chapel is a chapel no matter its state," she murmured.

As it turned out, and much to his chagrin, they had just made it to the old building before the skies opened up and rain poured down.

"'Tis good luck," Ada assured, eyeing the rainfall. "Most definitely good luck."

Greer didn't respond, but then it seemed she was tongue-tied.

"This was your future husband's idea," Cecille informed her daughter as Greer admired the torch-lit chapel strewn with wildflowers. She glanced at him and smiled. "I believe he called it wooing."

"'Tis beautiful." Greer blinked back tears when she looked at him. "Thank you."

"'Twas my pleasure." He winked at Duncan and Besse, who had helped him and Edmund collect the flowers. "'Twas a bit o' a group effort but, as all agreed, every warrior-hero should give his damsel in distress flowers."

"They should." Edmund pulled a flower from beneath his cloak and held it out to Ada. "For there is more than one damsel in distress in the room, aye? And I dare say, more than one warrior-hero?"

Ada's brows snapped together. "'Tis *their* moment, Sassenach, not yers."

"How come?" Besse frowned at her mother, having quite enjoyed Edmund's company while picking flowers. But then he had a way of making everything into an adventure. "I rather think ye deserve a flower, Ma."

"Aye," Duncan agreed, clearly just as taken with Edmund. "And he *did* save us, after all."

"Och, fine then." Although Ada snatched the flower from Edmund as if exasperated, a small smile hovered on her face when she nudged Teagan and Greer to get married already.

So it was, as rain pounded on the thatching overhead, that he wrapped a bit of MacLauchlin plaid around his and Greer's wrists and the holy man saw them married. Though Teagan had never said vows before nor put much ilk in love or marriage, he could admit saying the words that bound them together affected him. Almost as much as her saying them back.

Even the air around them felt different. Lighter somehow. As though joining with her in the eyes of God eased his burden. That being with a lass so kind and pure of heart allowed him to forgive himself just a wee bit. Mayhap it was knowing there *was* such goodness in this world. That, in some small way, good really *did* offset the evil.

"Ye may now kiss the bride," the holy man finally said once things were official.

"Aye," Teagan agreed, never so eager. He cupped Greer's cheeks and closed his mouth over hers.

"Bloody hell what the..." Ada exclaimed, interrupting the moment. She scowled at what had landed on her shoulder. "A *kitten*?"

"Och," Edmund exclaimed a moment later when a pup thumped down on his head.

Wide-eyed, Greer put a hand over her mouth, muffling laughter as her eyes went to the rafters overhead.

"Dinnae even say it," Ada warned Greer, handing the cat off to Besse.

"Say what?" Edmund gave the pup to Duncan and flinched when a heavy raindrop hit his cheek.

"Och, my apologies," the holy man exclaimed. "Animals tend to take shelter up there during rainfall, then inevitably discover how porous this building is. Now they but try to escape the wet coming through."

"I have heard of this happening," Adlin mused, with a twinkle in his eyes. "Though I've never seen it first-hand."

"'Tis all right," Greer assured the holy man, laughing merrily at Ada and Edmund, who, against the odds, were hit with one more of each animal. "'Tis actually *quite* perfect."

When Greer filled Teagan in on Ada claiming she would find love the day it rained cats and dogs, he couldn't help but chuckle as well. In truth, though, it wasn't beyond the realm of possibility as far as he could tell. Not with how Edmund looked at her. And while Ada seemed put off by him as a whole, Teagan couldn't help but notice how often they had ridden beside one another earlier.

"What would ye like to drink?" he asked Greer when they made their way into the tavern to celebrate. "Though they dinnae have wine, mayhap a spot of ale?"

"What about whisky?" she asked, surprising him. "I hear 'tis quite good in these parts."

"And quite strong," he warned.

"Even so." She smiled, making the roomful of people, if not the whole bloody country, fade away. "I think I would like to try some on my wedding day."

"Then so it shall be." He ordered two mugs, and they joined the others.

"Whisky, is it?" Cecille grinned at her daughter. "Good girl!"

Greer met her grin and sipped it only to flinch and cough.

"'Tis not bad," Greer managed, coughing again. "Quite good, actually."

"Aye, especially when served with food," Teagan recommended and saw to it.

As it happened, despite trouble brewing on the morrow, their wedding celebration was unforgettable. For the first time in longer than he could remember, Teagan not only smiled and laughed but danced. He felt alive in a way he hadn't for far too long. Present, when too often his mind drifted into the past.

"I cannae tell ye how good it is to see ye like this," Malcolm said at one point, sharing a dram with him. "Whilst I would have thought such change in so little time impossible, I'm living proof it happens. Greer is taming yer inner beasties, and 'tis a welcome sight, brother."

Malcolm *was* living proof, the deep love he'd found with Isabella, unquestionable. His eyes never strayed, and Teagan knew they never would. Their bond was too strong. Forged in a shared past. Unbreakable in a way Teagan hoped his and Greer's might someday be.

"Aye, Greer has made all the difference." Teagan couldn't take his eyes off of her as she danced with the bairns. "'Tis hard to explain..."

When he broke off, having no words for it, Malcolm clasped his shoulder. "Then dinnae try. Just live in the moment, here and now, and love her."

"I dinnae know much about love," he murmured out of habit, though the words didn't feel quite right on his tongue anymore.

"Ye know more than ye think." Malcolm noted how Greer glanced Teagan's way more often than not. "As does she."

Though the celebration went on for some time and Greer enjoyed her whisky, he, like most men there, refrained from drinking too much. It was best to keep a clear head and remain alert not only because of what loomed on the morrow but because they were so close to the border.

Eventually, he scooped his new wife up and carried her off to bed amid many cheers of goodwill.

"What a wonderful evening this has been," she murmured when he set her down in a small room with a single candle. "Better than any of my stories could have spun it."

"Somehow, I doubt that." He removed the ring of flowers from her head. "None tell a tale quite like ye."

When she smiled at him shyly, wondering what came next, he made things clear.

"'Twill not be what ye think this eve, lass." It would be bloody hard, but this could only go one way. "I willnae take ye when ye're in yer cups. 'Tis not how it should be our first time."

He bit back a smile at the look of disappointment in her eyes.

"Not to say yer wedding night doesnae still have some wooing ahead." He removed her belt and untied her dress, rallying his strength, praying his willpower held. But he wanted her to have something this night. An experience he suspected she'd never had before. "If ye'd like some more wooing, that is?"

"I cannot see it hurting," she said softly, a curious light in her eyes. "Though I will admit, now I wish I had not enjoyed your Scottish whisky so much."

"May those words never leave yer lips again," he admonished. "I wouldnae have had it any other way. 'Twas *yer* wedding, too, lass. Yer grand adventure and yer first taste of freedom. 'Twould have been a shame had ye not enjoyed every wee part of it." He cocked a crooked grin. "And trust me, whisky *is* verra much a part of a proper Scottish adventure."

"I tended to think so." Greer kept smiling, almost as if she couldn't help it. She rested her hand on his chest, her tongue bold, thanks to said whisky. "Though I do so look forward to a *full* Scottish adventure and all it entails."

"Soon enough, wife." Teagan crouched and removed her boots, then her hose. How he longed to run his hands up her soft thighs. To touch her wet center. "When the time is right." He lowered her dress to the floor, biting back a groan at the sight of her curves beneath her shift. "Until then, enjoy what I can offer ye now."

"And what would that be?" she whispered, toying with his tunic when he stood. "For, I can think of a few wedding gifts that would be suitable."

Whisky or not, he enjoyed the woman emerging in her.

"Let me show ye, lass." He pulled her close and cupped her cheek. "Let me show ye what a proper husband should be like."

Chapter Twenty-Two

GREER WAS CERTAIN all the whisky in the world could not dull her senses to the feel of Teagan's mouth against hers when he kissed her. Nor the rush of heat that pooled below when his kisses grew more insistent. Hungry in a way that made her knees go weak and the room tilt.

Nothing felt more erotic than his strong length against hers with naught but a thin chemise separating them. Nor anything more impactful than his hand trailing down the side of her neck so lightly every nerve ending sparked with awareness.

Eager to feel more of him, *see* more of him, she tugged on his tunic without realizing she did it. But then sensations came at her so fast it was impossible to control her own reactions. Her need to experience all he had to offer. All she suspected, *knew* he could make her feel. Wondrous things that had always felt so out of reach. So impossible in her world.

Understanding what she needed, he pulled his tunic off and tossed it aside, indeed giving her a remarkable wedding gift. She'd never seen a man with such well-defined muscles nor, sadly, one so scarred.

"Dear sweet Lord," she whispered hoarsely, both aroused and heartbroken at the same time. "What did they do to you?" She tried to touch him but shook too badly. "What did my people do to you?"

"'Tis just part of warfare, lass." He placed her trembling hand against his hard flesh. Over one of the more angry scars. "It no longer hurts."

"It does me." She blinked back tears. "I don't understand why men do this to each other. Why..."

When she broke off, too emotional to continue, he wrapped her in his arms and simply held her. Though she managed to hold herself together, it wasn't easy. His suffering triggered so much. Memories she'd long learned to suppress.

"Memories that have no place in this moment," she swore Margery whispered. "This is your time, Greer. Love him rather than cry over him. Be here, now, rather than there."

"I know," she whispered against his chest, not worried about him thinking her mad. "I will try."

She pulled back enough that she could see his scars again. This time she didn't shy away but touched them gently, soothingly, grateful each was healed. That each had, in its own way, allowed him to keep going. To be here now with her.

Gooseflesh rose on his skin, but he didn't stop her. Rather, he watched her as though wondering what she made of him. Not necessarily of the scars, either, but something deeper. Something she couldn't see with her eyes but feel with her heart. In some ways, he struck her as a wounded animal. Fearful how she might treat his broken state while at the same time eager to be whole again. To be seen for the man he once was.

She, however, saw him for who he was then and who he was now.

"You are exceptional," she whispered, meaning every word. "All of you, husband."

His tortured gaze lingered on her face a moment longer before he cupped her cheeks and kissed her again. Kissed her with a new kind of passion. An intensity born of having his soul laid bare. Being accepted despite her not knowing his sins.

Fortunately, he scooped her up before her knees gave out and laid her down gently on the cot. When he removed his boots, her heart leapt with anticipation. She saw the thick ridge straining against his breeches. How aroused he was.

So had he changed his mind? Would he make love to her after all?

It just so happened he did, but not like she thought he would. Instead, he kept his breeches on and came over her, his gaze so full of desire her breath caught.

"Ye are so bloody beautiful, Greer," he murmured, tracing her lips. "Yer mouth, so sweet." He trailed his fingers from her lips down her neck. "Yer neck so delicate."

Tingling pleasure uncurled everywhere at his light touch and impassioned words.

He brushed his lips across hers, then peppered kisses in the wake of his fingers, murmuring more endearments against her flesh. How soft her skin was, how perfect the slope of her shoulders. She stilled when his warm breath fanned her vulnerable skin, and he kissed the mounds of her cleavage.

Rather than pull down her chemise, his gaze returned to her face as his fingers wandered lower, exploring ever-so-slowly the curves of her breasts. She stopped breathing at the feel of him stroking and fondling her sensitive flesh while keeping their gazes locked. While letting her see the lust simmering in his eyes.

She arched into his touch when he pinched a nipple, then groaned when he used his mouth instead. When she began trembling, overwhelmed by sensation, he returned to her lips and kissed her all over again.

He repeated his slow sensual assault on her several times, arousing her so much, she was barely aware of him traveling lower until she felt his warm hand on her thigh. Until she felt his lips press against her belly. He slowly pushed her chemise up her legs, peppering kisses all the while.

When she began trembling again, he started all over at her lips, then her neck and breasts until she found herself pressing her hips against him in need. Eager for whatever he intended. Desperate for him to assuage the deep ache that had formed below. When, at last, his kisses made their way up her inner thighs, and his hot breath fanned her core, she nearly came off the bed.

In turn, he pushed her chemise around her waist and held her hips gently, keeping her in place. Giving her no time to think or feel embarrassed, he flicked his tongue deep into her soft folds. Her groan tangled with his at the sheer sensation that shot through her. The undulation of exquisite pleasure.

After that, there was no more trembling.

At least, not at first.

Rather, she melted beneath his ministrations.

He licked, kissed, and suckled. His fingers worked her sensitive, swollen flesh, touching and stroking, building her up. Then up some more. She fisted the blanket and struggled for air when he pressed first one, then two fingers into her while using his tongue in all sorts of creative ways.

She'd never felt anything like it. Ecstasy ebbed and flowed through her, building, and building. Higher and higher. Though frightening in its intensity, she couldn't fight it if she tried. Whatever it was came swiftly, ferociously, crawling through her veins. A delicious indescribable heat.

Fast, faster, so close, almost there.

She cried out and seized up when it crashed over her like a tidal wave, rushing from her center out to her fingertips. Frozen in limbo, she tried to breathe, speak, anything, but it was impossible. Rather, her body trembled again, before her muscles clenched and unclenched and she let go altogether.

Meanwhile, Teagan continued licking and stroking her softly, drawing out the wonderful sensations washing over her. Eventually, when she was well beyond satiated, he rested beside her and wrapped her in his arms. Lost, afloat somewhere she'd never been before, she nuzzled closer and inhaled the scent of his skin, never more content.

Satisfied and relaxed in a way she didn't think possible.

At some point, she must have drifted off because the next thing she knew, a knock came at the door, and sunlight shone in the window. Teagan was on his feet in an instant with a dagger in hand.

"Who goes there?" he said without opening the door.

"'Tis me, brother," Malcolm replied. "'Tis time."

Teagan opened the door. "What word have ye?"

"Only that they draw closer quickly, and we best ready ourselves."

"Aye." He nodded. "We will be right down."

"Oh, Lord," she whispered, trying not to panic. Moreover, trying to be as collected as those in her tales during times of distress.

"'Tis all right, lass." He shouldered into a tunic, calm as could be. "We willnae let anything happen to ye and yer friends."

"I'm more worried about you," she replied, yanking on a dress.

"All will be well." He cupped her shoulders and held her gaze. "Not only are Malcolm and I seasoned fighters, but the MacLomains are nae the sort to be defeated." He shook his head. "Not ever."

"Be that as it may." She tried to bank her fear. To be the brave heroine in her own tale. To make him proud. "I still worry."

"'Tis natural." He sat her on the bed, chatting away whilst putting on her hose and boots. A means, she realized, to distract her. "'Twill be over soon enough, then ye will have more confidence."

She nodded, hoping so, trying not to overthink things as he pulled on his boots and strapped on his weapons. Yet, she couldn't help but wonder. Would he gain more scars? Or would this be the day, defending her honor, that he received his mortal wound?

"Impossible," Margery would say. "If he's defending your honor, nothing will take him down. Surely you see that? Feel it in the way he looks at you?"

"'Tis fanciful indeed to think I alone would keep him safe," she countered.

"Then fanciful it is," Margery would exclaim. "For surely, you will." Her eyes would narrow at him in contemplation. "Honestly, based on his evident anticipation, I would say he's eager to battle Bartholomew." She'd shake her head. "And, quite frankly, I don't blame him."

As it turned out, she was right.

Greer could never have foreseen the horror that would come of that anticipation.

Chapter Twenty-Three

After Teagan was confident the lasses and children would be safe in the tavern and bid Greer farewell, he joined everyone just beyond the village.

"Though I wish we could travel further out," Edmund said, "'tis unwise to leave so many innocents undefended. So, 'tis here we must make our stand."

"'Tis a good place." Adlin eyed the thick woodland around them. "'Tis always better to fight among the trees than out in the open."

"Aye, Da." Tiernan grinned. "Especially when it comes to the Sassenach."

They were right, and many a Scotsman had figured that out. The English didn't do as well on terrain like this.

"There they are." Malcolm narrowed his eyes at the faint movement in the distance. "Tracking ye, just as Cecille hoped."

Teagan couldn't help but grin with anticipation. He longed for the moment he could finish off at least one of Greer's monsters. A monster, as they soon learned, who had a sizeable amount of men with him. Greer's cousin Alfred rode alongside Bartholomew, his expression hard to read.

"I dinnae see Randolph," Edmund muttered, switching to his inner Scot. "Where is the bloody bastard?"

Uneasy, Teagan scanned the Sassenach warriors and shook his head. "I dinnae see him either."

"Where is she, Scotsman?" Bartholomew called out. Despite being confronted with a line of Scottish warriors comparable to his own, the Englishman looked down his nose at Teagan. "Where is my wife?"

"Ye mean *my* wife," he called back. "For we were married last night, Sassenach."

Though fury blazed in Bartholomew's gaze, he held his ground. "You will not incite me with lies."

"'Tis no lie," the holy man called out. Robed and all, he'd insisted on being there lest Bartholomew needed proof. "I married them myself under God's eyes. Mistress Greer is wed to Teagan MacLauchlin, and ye, good sir, are nae welcome here!"

"Why should I believe you, Scot?" Disgust flashed in Bartholomew's eyes. "Bible or no, you are every bit the barbarian your countrymen are." His gaze homed in on Teagan again. "Return Greer to me, and I will not bring the wrath of England down on you and yours."

"The wrath of England?" Edmund guffawed, snorting. He peered around as if looking for more men behind Bartholomew. "Have ye all that at yer back then? For, it doesnae look it."

"Traitor," Bartholomew ground out. "Was the safety of your people, your family, worth all this? These filthy Scots?"

Rather than respond to the Englishman's taunts, Edmund slid a look Teagan's way. "What say ye, friend? If he isnae going to be run off, might we get around to battling?"

"Aye, I'm all for it." He cocked a brow at Adlin and Tiernan. "What about ye? More talk or more fighting?"

"There isnae any reasoning with ignorance." Adlin unsheathed his blade. "So, I say fighting." He considered the line of Sassenach. "My guess is more will flee than fight."

"Aye," Tiernan concurred, noting the unease in the eyes of Bartholomew's men. "We willnae see too much strife this day."

"There ye have it." Teagan grinned at Edmund, raising his voice so that all heard, so damn eager his fingers twitched on his blade. "Fighting it is!"

"Unreasonable heathens," Bartholomew shot back. He unsheathed his blade as the wall of Scots cried their various war cries and charged those who thought themselves superior, on Scottish soil no less.

Teagan spurred his horse with but one target in mind. It seemed Bartholomew felt the same because moments later, they clashed swords before the Englishman swung down, determined to battle afoot. With good reason, too. Greer was right. He excelled with a blade, and fighting this way gave him more options.

As men fought around them, they circled one another, gauging each other's weaknesses, be it in one's grip or footwork. Unfortunately, he detected none in the Sassenach. In fact, the moment he and Bartholomew engaged one another, he knew things wouldn't go as smoothly as he'd hoped. That said, he needed to dislodge his opponent's weapon. Where he doubted the Englishman had brute strength, his sword was very much an extension of his arm.

Tuning out everything around them, Teagan focused solely on the rapid movements of Bartholomew's sword, sensing, yet again, no weaknesses. Even his footwork was flawless.

Sometimes the Englishman drove him back. Other times, he had the upper hand.

"Ye need to get that blade out of his hand soon, brother," Keenan would persist. "If not, he will wear ye down, and that will be the end of it."

He was right. Time was limited.

Yet everything he threw at the man, Bartholomew countered. The Sassenach spun away after one incredibly close thrust only to come at Teagan all that much harder. Sweat broke out on his brow. His muscles strained. They swirled, evaded, their movements swift, endless, and tiring.

Slowly but surely, a pompous grin slithered onto Bartholomew's face as he drove Teagan back. Then back some more. "Did you really think yourself better than me, Scot?" He chuckled. "Surely now, you see the error of your ways. The foolishness of your actions." The Sassenach cocked his head as though thinking about that. "But then perhaps not." He flicked his sword even faster, laughing madly before he dislodged Teagan's blade at last. "For you Scottish animals are—"

"No, stop!" Greer cried, drawing Bartholomew's attention away just long enough for Teagan to scoop up his sword.

"Bloody *hell*," he cursed when he realized Greer had grabbed hold of Duncan, who, dagger in hand, obviously thought to come to their aid.

Just like she'd done at the beginning, Greer took up position in front of the lad. Only this time, she had a pompous, bloodthirsty Bartholomew barreling down on her.

"N-nay," Alfred roared, stepping in front of her. Though trembling like a leaf, he held his blade at the ready and narrowed his eyes on Bartholomew. "Stop r-right there, I say! Stop in the name of all that is g-good!"

Suddenly immobile, caught in a memory, a violent moment in time, Teagan could barely think, let alone take action. Just like that, because of Alfred's stance, he had returned to that horrible day. Saw the horrors in the village. The broken bodies of women and children. Their lifeless eyes staring at the sky. The pure degradation left in the wake of living, breathing men, turned monsters. The ruthlessness and evil of which people were capable.

Worse yet, he saw the man on the woman once more.

The brutality she had suffered.

Somehow that memory merged with Bartholomew shoving Alfred aside and grabbing Greer.

The two realities became one, and Teagan saw pure red.

Felt pure rage.

He heard a furious roar from far off and somehow knew it was him.

He had made that tortured sound.

He had become the monster.

Teagan had no idea when he moved, only that he must have because, the next thing he knew, he'd disarmed Bartholomew and pulled him away. Away from Greer, just like he had pulled the man away from that poor woman years ago.

"Ye bloody beast," he swore, speaking to both the man from his past and Bartholomew. "Ye'll not hurt her again," he ground out. "Ye'll not hurt any of them."

Somewhere in the distance, he heard Adlin wondering if they should stop him, and Edmund and Malcolm unanimously saying *no*. None of it mattered, though. Nothing could stop him from unleashing pure hell on Bartholomew with his bare fists.

"Remember ye are nae alone, little brother," Keenan whispered into his mind, a voice of reason amid the chaos. Amid sheer unbridled hatred. "Ye've a wee bairn and the lass ye love watching ye."

"Love?" Punch. Punch. Punch. "I know nothing of love."

"Aye, ye do, or ye wouldnae have felt so strongly then nor now," Keenan would reply. "Ye couldnae feel such heartbreaking rage if ye didnae know love verra well."

"He's right," Greer whispered into his mind.

"Ye're right there, lass." Punch. Punch. "So ye cannae be in my mind."

"She can because she loves ye," Keenan would say. "She can because she understands yer ability to love."

"Love?" He stopped punching and gripped Bartholomew's tunic, trying to focus. "What do I know of..."

All of a sudden, his vision snapped into focus, and he saw the groaning Englishman beneath him. Not bloodied beyond recognition quite yet but definitely struggling.

"I *do* know of love," he murmured at last, seeing very clearly indeed. "Ye, however, Sassenach, know no such thing."

With that, he did the only thing he could, and it was not what anyone would have expected.

Chapter Twenty-Four

Greer blinked when Teagan rolled away from Bartholomew and braced his head in his hands. All she could focus on was Teagan as Ada pulled Duncan away. He was all she could see. Yet when she tried to go to him, her legs gave way, and she sank to her knees.

"I know you," she whispered.

Her voice sounded far away. As though it were not her own.

Every punch that Teagan landed on Bartholomew brought her further and further back. The torture in his actions. The pure rage. Closer and closer to something she'd hoped to forget. "I know you."

As though from a great distance, blades rang out as men battled. Axes hurled through the air. Daggers whipped. Grunts of pain echoed. She was vaguely aware of Alfred standing over Bartholomew. Of his barely stuttered words promising him a swift journey to hell. Then a harsh thrust when he drove his sword into their enemy.

Like her, Teagan was barely aware of the chaos surrounding them. The roars of fury and cries of victory. Rather, he had gone somewhere in his mind, grappling with something in his past.

Then it all spun away.

One moment she saw him sitting there, the next, she stared out a cracked window in another time and place. Her heart thundered. Her mouth went bone dry. Horrified, she strained to see in the dim light, praying she saw wrong. Praying her mind played tricks on her. Doing her best to keep her violent sobs quiet.

"Darling," her mother said from far off. "Darling Greer, you *must* come back to me. We *must* go."

She blinked, trying to see past the memory. Past her terror and gut-wrenching guilt. Thankfully, her mother kept talking, coaxing her forth, until she finally snapped into focus. When had her mother knelt in front of her? When had she gripped her shoulders?

When had the English retreated?

"I…she," she mouthed, trying to find her voice, trying so very hard to be in the present. "*He.*"

"Yes, he's gone." Mother brought a skin of water to her lips and urged her to drink. "Bartholomew is no longer a threat." Understanding that what had just happened had triggered Greer's violent past, her mother blinked back tears. "But your uncle is not gone, sweet daughter. He's en route to MacLauchlin Castle and your sister, Julianna, so we *must* stop him."

"Julianna?" she whispered. "The MacLauchlins?"

"Yes." Her mother wiped tears from Greer's face she hadn't realized had fallen. "We must make haste and stop him, so we need to go now." She cupped Greer's cheeks and held her gaze. "Do you hear me, daughter? We must rally our courage and press on. You *must* continue your grand adventure. You must be the heroine, yes?"

"Yes," she managed, frightened for her sister. For Teagan's people.

"I have ye, lass," Teagan said, somehow no longer holding his head but crouched in front of her. "I'm here now. I'm sorry I wasnae before…" Pain saturated his gaze. "That I couldnae be there for ye sooner." He cupped her cheek. "But I am now."

Greer nodded and whispered, "I know."

He cupped her other cheek and searched her eyes. "Aye?"

She bit her lower lip and kept nodding. "Yes."

He pressed his forehead to hers, a means to connect with her, to show her how much he cared before his gaze returned to her face. "Can ye stand?"

"I think so."

She thanked him, grateful when he helped both her and her mother to their feet.

"Are you all right?" Finally gathering her wits, Greer frowned at his wounded knuckles. "I can dress that for you."

"Nay, 'tis fine." His brow furrowed, and he kept his hand at her waist. "Are ye well enough to ride?"

"I am," she assured, gaining her footing. She looked around only to realize most were already gone. "Are you sure Randolph heads for your castle? Could it be Edmund's men simply led him astray?"

"Nay, his men went in the opposite direction of MacLauchlin Castle," he replied. "So, he's definitely heading for Julianna."

"Then we should go." Her gaze fell to Bartholomew, her feelings raw but not for him. He'd reaped what he sowed. "Someone should see him properly buried."

"The holy man said he would see to it." Teagan saw her mother onto her horse before helping Greer onto his and swinging up behind her. "'Twill be hard riding."

Though her mind continued going in circles, still partly in the past, she grew more aware by the moment.

"Good," Margery would have said. "Enough with all that back there. 'Tis time to help your husband and new friends and live the life you were destined for."

"As are you," she whispered.

"As was I," Margery corrected, putting emphasis on the past tense. "Now focus on the here and now so that you might make it home to MacLauchlin Castle."

Although the rain had let up last night, the ground was still slick underfoot and the rivers swollen, so traveling wasn't as easy as it might have been. Even so, they moved fast enough that there was little time to speak with Teagan about what had happened back there.

Because something *had* happened.

What, exactly, remained just out of reach.

Regardless, they moved right along and, fortunately, caught up with the others at the next village.

"Malcolm's gone on ahead, aye?" Teagan asked Edmund when he didn't spy his brother. "Scouting?"

"Aye," Edmund confirmed.

Teagan helped Greer down, only for Ada to embrace her tightly.

"Is everything all right?" Greer frowned and looked around, trying not to envision the worst. "Where are the children?"

"Here and safe, thanks to you, Teagan, and Alfred." Ada shook her head when she pulled back, referring to Greer's flashback. "I'm so sorry we couldnae stay on when ye needed me most, but Edmund insisted we keep moving. That Bartholomew's men could turn back at any moment."

"He was right to insist such," she assured. "I'm sorry I snuck out of the tavern like that."

Greer had snuck out to go to Teagan's aid if need be, not realizing Duncan had done the same determined to fight alongside the men. Suffice it to say, she'd happened upon the boy just in the nick of time before he rushed into battle.

"Though 'twas trying all the way around," Ada replied. "I amnae sorry ye snuck out and came upon my lad."

Ada shook her head at Duncan, who had just joined them. His eyes widened on Teagan.

"Did ye see it?" He blinked at Teagan in wonder before he looked at Greer. "Did ye see how the fairies came to yer warrior-hero's aid in battle? How their fairy fire protected his blade, then gave him the good wisdom to be a better man than his enemy?"

"I saw it from the window," Besse echoed in awe, though she couldn't possibly have. But brothers and sisters stuck together. "I saw it clear as day!"

When Teagan and Greer looked at Ada in confusion, she was sure to look impressed. "Aye, how could they not see the sparks on

Teagan's blade when he fought his greatest foe?" She perked a brow. "Or when he chose to spare his mortal enemy rather than become like him and slay him ruthlessly?"

Ah, so the metal clashing caused sparks, and imaginations took over.

"'Twas *quite* impressive," Duncan praised, eyeing Alfred with newfound respect as he helped with the horses. "As was Sir Alfred's valor in finally putting the beast out of his misery."

"I could not agree more," Greer's mother concurred. "As always, I'm proud to call him kin." She shared a knowing look with Greer. "He is most unlike my brother."

"Yes, he is." She looked at Teagan. "Speaking of kin, will we press on? There are still a few hours of daylight left."

"Aye, I will continue on with the MacLomains," he responded. "Ye and yers will stay here for the eve where 'tis safer."

"No," she and her mother said at the same time. They glanced at each other, understanding one another perfectly.

"If my daughter and your kin are in danger," Mother went on, "I prefer to press on with you and help any way I can."

"As do I." Greer couldn't imagine being anywhere but by Teagan's side at this point. Yes, it was quick and might make little sense to some, but it was true. Not only was he her husband, but they were connected in a way her mind and heart struggled to make sense of. "I go where you go, husband."

Teagan frowned in concern, no doubt worried about her episode earlier. Her state of mind. "Are ye sure?"

"Yes." She nodded, never so certain of anything. "I need to be part of this final leg of the journey."

While remaining by his side felt crucial, she also wanted to be there when they faced off with her uncle. In a strange way, it felt like facing her past. She didn't want to tremble and hide in helpless cowardly terror anymore but meet her demons head-on. Monsters she hadn't realized until this morning still haunted her so much. She might not be able to wield a blade yet, but there were other ways to slay her demons.

"Sadly, I must stay here with my bairns," Ada said on a sigh, ignoring Duncan's groan of dismay. She shook her head at Greer. "After what happened earlier, I cannae risk their safety."

"Nor should ye." Teagan looked at Edmund. "Malcolm and I have enough fighting men thanks to the MacLomains staying on. Ye should remain here and watch over Ada and her bairns until we send word all is well."

"Are ye sure?" Edmund frowned, despite his obvious relief. He clearly wanted to help but, at the same time, didn't want Ada and the children left alone.

"Ye dinnae need to do that," Ada argued.

"'Tis not about need, lass," Edmund winked at Duncan, "but about being here to battle alongside yer lad if need be."

"Thank ye, good sir." Duncan rested a hand on the hilt of an imaginary dirk sheathed at his waist. "'Tis well past time I fight alongside an English-Scot."

Greer bit back a smile at the less derogatory term.

"Och, I dinnae need protecting," Ada muttered. She kissed Greer on the cheek and wished her well before ushering her children toward the village. Not before she had the final word, though.

"If ye must," Ada called over her shoulder, "come keep being our bloody hero, Sassenach!"

"But of course, darling," Edmund called back, sounding properly English just to irritate her. He grinned and tipped an imaginary hat to Greer, Teagan, and Cecille before he sauntered after Ada, muttering, "Ye feisty wench," under his breath.

"So all is as well as a raging storm can be with those two," Mother said with amusement. She shook her head, praising the potential romance. "Though there *is* something to be said for never having a dull moment."

"A raging storm, to be sure." Greer grinned. "But it *did* rain cats and dogs, so there's always hope."

"Indeed!" Adlin said upon approach. Undoubtedly a chipper soul by nature, he smiled. "And it certainly doesnae do that every day."

"No, it does not." Greer got the feeling he would get along well with Ada. They shared that same special something that made them unique.

"I've heard word of Sassenach activity ahead," Adlin informed them. "If we press on, we could intercept them within hours."

"Do you think 'tis my brother?" her mother asked.

"'Tis impossible to know." Adlin's brow swept up. "But well worth investigating, aye?"

"Aye," Teagan agreed.

As they learned a few hours later, they had no idea just how worth investigating it would really be. More worthy, as it turned out, than any of them could have ever imagined.

Chapter Twenty-Five

"THERE THEY ARE." Teagan crouched behind a copse of bushes with the others and narrowed his eyes on the Sassenach encampment. "The bloody fools settle on Scottish soil as if they own it." He shook his head at Malcolm, who had rejoined them a while back. "They have nerve. I will give them that."

"You mean my brother has nerve," Cecille said softly, narrowing her eyes as well. "But then, like Bartholomew, he thinks himself above your countrymen."

"So, how will we go about this?" Greer cocked a brow at Teagan, clearly wanting a role in this. "What can I do?"

"Yes," Alfred joined them, "w-what can we do?"

If he wasn't mistaken, Alfred's stutter had lessened some. Especially since he downed Bartholomew.

Teagan shook his head, not sure how he wanted to go about this yet. Though tempted to say he would rather Greer stay out of harm's way, he knew better. Since this morning's battle, and whatever traumatic event it brought her back to, she needed this. He sensed her ready to face her demons. Slay her dragons.

He would never forget the moment her pain pulled him free of his stupor. Her tortured expression had matched his inner angst. It had broken him out of his flashback so he could get to her. Soothe her. Help any way he could.

Since then, he had wondered where she'd been.

Why she whispered that she knew him.

What had happened? What terrorized her so much that her legs gave way when she tried to reach him? Because she had. He felt it despite his own horrific stupor. Then, despite being rendered immobile, she *still* pulled him free of his demons, the dark place he'd been, hinting at a deep connection betwixt them. One beyond the desire they had shared the night before. If what they'd shared could be called mere desire.

It had felt like so much more, though he'd yet to lay with her.

He could still taste her sweet juices and smell her honeyed scent. Still hear her throaty groans. See her beautiful body arching in pleasure. Still imagine her peaking for the first time. Going somewhere she'd never gone before. Feeling things he longed to make her feel time and time again.

"How do ye want to go about this?" Adlin asked Teagan and Malcolm, joining them as well. He looked at Cecille. "For 'tis yer brother, aye, lass?"

"'Tis," she confirmed, considering the ample amount of men Randolph had with him. She looked at Greer. "You say you want to help. What did you have in mind?"

"Avoiding too much bloodshed," Greer replied readily enough. "And retrieving the gem we both know he carries, for he would not trust it out of his sight."

Cecille looked at her with surprise. "Then, you do not want him to keep it?"

"I wished him to keep it when he remained in England." Greer shook her head. "Now that his greed and pettiness has driven him to go after my sister, I don't want him to keep much of anything."

Approval lit Cecille's eyes. "That sounds quite specific in a roundabout way, daughter."

"Oh, 'tis, Mother." She glared at Randolph, likely recalling all too well what she'd suffered at his hands. "Concise, indeed."

"I ken yer desire to help but," Teagan began before Greer cut him off.

"If you understand my desire to help, then there should be no buts." Her warm yet suspiciously devious gaze met his. "I can distract him whilst you see to business."

With that, before he could argue or stop her, she was gone, with Alfred in pursuit.

"Hell and damnation," he cursed.

"You have awoken something in her, Scotsman." Cecille's concerned gaze remained locked on Greer as she made her way into the encampment. "And I'm not sure if that's a good or bad thing at the moment."

"Och," he muttered. Very much a bad thing.

He went to stand, but Malcolm yanked him back down, put a finger to his mouth, and gestured in Greer's direction. It seemed she had a plan, and Alfred played right along.

"Uncle," she called out. When she staggered a little, Alfred took her elbow, offering her stability. She put the back of her hand to her forehead when Randolph's men stood and unsheathed their weapons. "Please, Uncle, I need your help."

"Smart girl," Cecille whispered, despite her obvious tension. Her gaze cut to Teagan and Malcolm. "You best be ready to take them all down at a moment's notice."

"'Tis *bloody* foolish," Teagan cursed under his breath for no other reason than his heart was in his throat with every step Greer took. Just one strike, one whip of a dagger or swipe of a blade, and she would be gone. Lost to him as quickly as he found her.

"'Tis bloody brave," Malcolm praised as Randolph stood.

Though he drew his own blade, the Englishman gestured that his men stand down.

"What's going on?" Randolph looked from Greer to Alfred and frowned. "Did you defeat the Scotsman? What happened?" He looked around. "Where is everyone else? Bartholomew?"

"I..." Greer inhaled a ragged breath. Her hand fluttered over her chest in distress. "I had no choice." She shook her head. "This is not what I wanted, but I had no choice." She sniffled as though crying. "Why would I want to leave such wealth? Such a promising life?"

"*'Twas* hard to believe." Randolph kept his weapon at the ready and eyed the darkness around him. "Where is your aunt? My sister?" He scowled at Alfred. "Tell me that damnable Scot is finished!"

"That would be ye, I imagine," Adlin said out of the corner of his mouth to Teagan. "It seems ye made quite the impression, lad."

"Yes, he did," Cecille agreed. "And may he make more of one on my blasted brother before all is said and done."

"Why is she doing this?" Teagan shook his head, barely able to think straight with Greer in so much danger. While he knew she faced her demons, this seemed like too much. Out of control.

"Because she's on a much-needed grand adventure," Cecille reminded, her gaze pained when she looked at her daughter. "Or should I say, finally breaking free from all that held her back? Fighting her oppressors the only way she knows how?"

"Yet ye sit here so calmly," he grumbled.

"You have no idea how I sit here," Cecille's voice wobbled with emotion. "All I know is Greer cannot go forward without going back. Nor can she free herself without facing her fears. Even if those fears are in the form of an uncle who's but a fraction of the monsters she's seen, yet a monster all the same."

"Wise words," Adlin murmured, listening to Alfred's explanation that he got Greer away from the Scot, but it hadn't been easy. The fighting had been overwhelming. He wasn't sure who lived or died. All he knew was Greer wanted to flee, so he saw her safely here.

"For if ever a lass is facing her fears, 'tis your wife, Teagan." Adlin nodded with approval. "Ye should be verra proud."

He was, but that didn't make this any easier. He envisioned Greer coming out of her shell as time went on, not thrusting her shell aside altogether and doing something so bold and dangerous. But then he shouldn't be all that surprised considering how quickly she was blossoming. How eager she seemed to break free.

"So, you managed to break off from your mother and the Scotsman?" Randolph went on, responding to whatever tale Greer and Alfred spun. "Because they chose to fight Bartholomew when he came for you?"

"I tried to sooner." Greer inhaled a choppy breath and staggered a little as though exhausted. "But that man…" She released a broken sob. "That Scottish beast was just as you claimed these Scots to be." Another broken sob. "He did things to me…"

"Oh, goodness, child!" Randolph's gaze skirted over his men, his worry clearly not for what she'd suffered but that her reputation might be tarnished. If that happened, she could no longer make a beneficial marriage.

"Come sit and rest." Randolph urged her to sit beside him, coaxing her to say what he wished. To retell her tragedy to suit his needs. "Tell me what happened, dear niece. Tell me how these awful Scots nearly ruined you, but alas, did not have you in the end."

Adlin snorted softly and shook his head at Cecille and Teagan. "He really is a bit of a nefarious character, is he not?"

"He is a bit of something," Cecille replied, disgusted. "He's a tedious, horrid man."

"Well, of course, I fought them off before Bartholomew and his men arrived," Greer said in response to her uncle's statement about the Scots not ultimately having her. Her eyes widened, and her hand went to her heart. She sounded wounded and distressed. "Surely, such is not in question? Surely, you do not think I would allow one of these heathens to…" She squeezed her eyes shut as if truly pained before she looked at Randolph again. "I hope you don't think poorly toward my good honor?"

"Oh, but she *is* my daughter," Cecille praised on a whisper. "Just *listen* to her."

Teagan was. Closely. And was impressed.

Nevertheless.

Was Randolph buying it? Or was he biding his time? There was no trusting the man. He was an equally efficient actor. A genuine liar.

"'Tis going too smoothly," Malcolm murmured, as though reading his mind. "I dinnae like it."

"Nor I." Teagan narrowed his eyes on the men surrounding Randolph, then those at nearby campfires. "Something is amiss."

"'Tis," Malcolm agreed. His gaze skirted the wood line, his instincts as attuned as Teagan's. "What, though?"

"What indeed?" Cecille frowned. "Randolph seems quite taken by Greer's tale."

"He does," Teagan eyed the Sassenach again, "*seems* that way."

"I would never think any ill-will toward your good honor, my dear niece," Randolph said, pulling them back to the ongoing conversation. "I would, however, wonder at the man who stumbled into my camp early this morn who told a different story entirely."

Greer barely had a chance to look surprised before Randolph yanked her to her feet, put a knife to her throat, and narrowed his eyes on the dark woodland around him.

"Show yourself, sister," he called out. "Show yourself, you traitorous bitch!"

"Here I am," Cecille called back, standing without hesitation.

Teagan and Malcolm started in different directions, doing what they often did during war. Hoped for the best but prepared for the worst without saying a word.

While Teagan's terror for Greer cut to his core, his instincts kept him moving. Thinking clearly. Covering ground stealthily. Quickly and without sound.

Randolph would never see him or his brother coming.

"I'm here, brother," Cecille called out again, heading Randolph's way. "Let her go."

Her brother chuckled and eyed the forest, warning his men to be at the ready. They were likely surrounded, but not to worry, he still had the upper hand.

Meanwhile, Alfred went for his blade.

Randolph narrowed his eyes. "I would not do that." His dark gaze flickered to his sister. "Tell whoever you have with you to throw down their weapons and step into the light, and I will let Greer go." He pressed the blade tighter to Greer's throat. "Otherwise, your daughter dies."

"Dies over my dead body," Teagan nearly ground out but bit his tongue and stayed to the shadows, drawing ever closer, just like Malcolm did from the other side.

"Throw down your weapons," Cecille called out obediently, her voice shaky. Unlike Greer, she wasn't acting, but he didn't blame her. Randolph pressed the blade so tightly against Greer now, blood trickled down her neck.

The same delicate neck he'd worshiped the night before. The same soft, vulnerable skin. His heart slammed into his throat at the thought of never tasting her again. Never hearing her soft voice. Seeing the compassion in her eyes when she cried over his scars.

"Nay," he cursed, unable to hold back anymore. Knowing, without question, he was losing control. But the thought of losing her made him physically ill. Lethally enraged. Unable to see reason.

Even as he knew full well he wasn't close enough to them yet.

Nonetheless, he aimed his dagger, ready to throw, only for someone else to whip two of theirs first. Not Malcolm either. Nay, these were different, the marksmanship flawless. One pinned the exact spot just above Randolph's elbow that made him drop the knife to Greer's throat. The second sliced clean through the side of Randolph's neck.

A sizeable warrior around Adlin's age with silvery black hair and familiar blue eyes stepped into the light. His identity, as it happened, stunned every last person there, including, interestingly enough, Randolph's warriors.

Chapter Twenty-Six

GREER BLINKED, NOT sure she saw correctly. Could it be? Was it really him?

"Stand down!" Their hero pointed his blade at Randolph's men before they thought to take action. "You know who I am, so you know who's in charge now."

Teagan joined Greer and pulled her close, his blade at the ready even as he held a scrap of plaid to her wounded neck.

"Phillip?" her mother whispered, wide-eyed. Her hand fluttered to her stomach. "Is that you?"

But of course, it was. He might have changed some, hardened to be sure, but there was no mistaking her father.

"Yes." Phillip's pained gaze went from Greer to her mother. "'Tis me." His eyes lingered on her a moment before returning to Randolph's men. *His men now.* Being married to Mother made him next in line to inherit Randolph's estate. "Sheath your weapons and stand down. If not, the Scots surrounding you will finish you off."

Right on time, Teagan and Malcolm's men, along with the MacLomains, melted out of the darkness. All grew very quiet. Crackling fires became deafening and gazes warier by the moment as men sized each other up. How far would their opponent go? Was this a fight to the death? Sweat pearled on foreheads. Jaws clenched. Gazes grew more untrusting still.

Would mayhem unleash?

Was there yet more blood to be shed?

Thankfully, in the end, one by one, Randolph's men sheathed their blades, many clearly relieved. In truth, based on the looks her uncle received as he lay dying, he hadn't been overly favored. But then, if he left his estate and without doubt many of these men's families undefended, it was no wonder.

Confident all was well, her father looked at Greer's throat with concern.

"Greer," he said softly, closing the distance. "Are you all right, daughter?"

"Yes," she managed, still coping with the shock of seeing him. "'Tis but a scratch." She looked from Mother to Father. "How are you here? I thought you…"

"Died," her mother said hoarsely, finishing her sentence when she trailed off.

"Not dead." He pulled her mother into a tight embrace. "But very much alive."

"Thank God." Mother pressed her cheek to his chest and embraced him just as tightly. "Thank our dear, merciful savior."

Greer swallowed hard and nodded that she was okay when Teagan removed the cloth and eyed her wound.

"I'm all right." In fact, she was better than she'd been in a long time. Not only because her father was here but because of what had just happened. The courage and freedom she'd felt taking action like that. Even if her uncle had known things were off from the beginning, she'd gotten the ball rolling.

"Daughter." Her father reeled her into his and her mother's embrace. "How I have missed you both. All of you."

While still somewhat hurt and confused over his sudden departure, she didn't feel as strongly as she had before. Truth told, it hardly mattered anymore. What mattered was him being here now. Because whatever happened, there could be no doubt he loved her dearly.

"We need to talk," he murmured. "All of us. So that you might understand."

"Yes." Mother wiped away a tear as she pulled back. "We most certainly do."

"There's a village close by." Father crouched and rummaged through Randolph's pockets until he found the gem. "We will rest there for the eve." He stood and addressed his men. "'Tis your choice if you stay on at my estate. If you do, expect things to change. As many of you already know, I'm not the man your former liege was." He shook his head. "No man, woman, or child, be they Scottish or English, will be kept under my care unless they wish to be there. All will earn fair wages."

He looked at Alfred and nodded with pride.

"Whilst I'm in Scotland seeing to my family, Alfred will be in charge." He clasped Alfred's shoulder. "He's proven himself a true warrior in every sense of the word." Emotion flashed in his eyes as he looked at him. "You have my deepest gratitude for protecting my eldest daughter as you have."

"'Twas my h-honor." Alfred straightened and looked at the men. "As 'twill be my honor overseeing your estate and the good men who protect it."

She was relieved to see so many nod their heads in turn. To see so many of a different mind than their former liege.

"I would suggest you head back tonight," her father counseled Alfred. "'Twas foolish of Randolph to leave our estate so undefended and bring our men here. 'Tis too dangerous."

Alfred nodded. "Yes, m'lord."

Alfred embraced Cecille goodbye, then Greer.

"One of these days I will visit, and we will talk some, yes?" Greer smiled at Alfred, never so grateful. Sad that it had taken her all this time to get to know him better. To push beyond her demons and see him for the hero he was. Had always been. "I think it long past time we became friends."

"I would like that," he replied without nary a stutter. He nodded at Teagan, then looked at her again. "I wish you only the best, Mistress Greer. A lifetime of happiness."

"Thank you," she whispered, teary despite herself. "As do I, you."

As Alfred and his men made ready to leave, the MacLomains said their goodbyes as well.

"This is where we part ways, I'm afraid." Adlin clasped hands with Teagan and Malcolm and smiled warmly at Greer. "Wishing you and your new husband the verra best. Until we meet again, might you enjoy Clan MacLauchlin and your bonnie new country."

"Many thanks." She smiled at Teagan. "I cannot imagine it any other way."

They said goodbye to Tiernan as well and bid them all farewell.

"I will send a man to let Ada and Edmund know all is well," Adlin assured, swinging onto his horse.

"Please do," her father replied, having evidently followed a great deal of their adventure from afar. "Tell Edmund that whilst the men who traveled with him to the border were unable to detour Randolph, they remain unscathed. Also, he's not to worry over his estate and kin. We will see them protected, and any rumors of treason quelled."

"Aye." Adlin nodded. "I'll see the message delivered straight away." He winked at Greer. "Best to put his mind at ease so he can enjoy his eve with Ada and the wee ones."

With that, he and his men left, as did everyone else after Randolph was buried, and a prayer said over his grave. They would stay at the village for the night, then arrive at MacLauchlin Castle on the morrow.

"How fare ye, lass?" Teagan murmured in her ear as they traveled. "Truly?"

"Good," she replied. "Very good, actually…and looking forward to talking with you later."

"Aye?" he asked curiously. "What about?"

"Things long past needing to be discussed," she said vaguely, not wanting to do this on horseback in the dark but where she could see him. "Things I want you to know about me."

"Aye, then," he said softly, hesitant. "Mayhap, I've things to share as well."

"I hope so," she whispered, glad to hear it. Because she knew it had to do with what happened that morning. Demons that needed to be confronted once and for all.

As it turned out, though very small, the tavern in the next village had room enough for the four of them. Malcolm and their men continued on to let everyone at MacLauchlin Castle know all was well and their enemies no more.

Thunder rumbled in the distance as she, Teagan, and her parents finally settled in front of a fire with a drink. This time she opted for ale, if for no other reason than to keep her head clear.

"Are you sure that's the only reason?" Margery would have said with a twinkle in her eyes. "Or could it be you wish to finally consummate your marriage?"

She bit back a smile, glad to hear Margery again but, at the same time, not alarmed she hadn't heard from her more today. That she seemed to be stepping back and nudging Greer to take the lead. To face things on her own.

"So you see, Cecille," her father said in conclusion, having explained his whereabouts. "I did what I thought best to keep you and our daughters safe until the time was right." His pained gaze turned Greer's way. "I cannot tell you how hard it was leaving you behind, daughter. Worse yet, not saying goodbye." He shook his head. "But 'twas far too risky. Your husband would have sent word I was there, and Randolph would have pursued straight away when I did not return."

"Had that happened, you would never have made it to Scotland," Mother surmised. "And never had the coin to start over nor the leverage we needed to get Greer back."

Though Greer would have snuck away with him, she knew better than to voice it. Joining him would have brought her husband and Randolph's wrath down on him even quicker, and that was the last thing she would have wanted. Not for her father, mother, or sister, for it would have affected them all.

"I must say, Ena was very convincing," her mother mused, referring to the old woman she'd met in the Scottish village who claimed Father had died. She shook her head at Phillip. "Was that really so necessary?" Her eyes welled, but she blinked it away. "It broke my heart."

"'Twas not my decision, love, but Ena and her good husband's," he said on a sigh. "As I told you, 'twas not easy for her to keep the whole truth from you, but she did it with good reason. She would not risk me being discovered until I did what needed to be done."

"Which was going back for our Greer," her mother murmured. "A worthy cause, indeed."

"Yes, once the jewels were secure and I knew you and Julianna had what you needed, I headed back." He shook his head. "I could not linger in the Scottish village knowing Greer was all alone back in England, and Ena knew that. She also knew if someone caught wind of me being alive, it could very easily lead back to the gems and her people."

Mother nodded, understanding what he didn't say as well.

"'Twas also for the best I not get my hopes up but remain realistic," Mother deduced. "After all, you were putting your life on the line every step you took in both Scotland and England."

"Yes," her father said softly. "Seen clearly enough."

Greer blinked back tears, not only because he'd come back for her but because of the trouble he had run into before he got out of Scotland. At the hands of Scottish pirates no less.

Teagan shook his head. "'Tis a wonder ye survived."

"No doubt." Mother squeezed her father's hand. "You were always very clever, though."

"'Twas just a matter of thinking like them and proving myself useful." Father shook his head. "And what's more useful than a *Sassenach* who could fight well and help them get closer to my countrymen? Steal from them more readily?" His eyes grew haunted. "'Twas not easy betraying my own, but if it meant getting Greer away from tyrants and back to her kin, I was willing to do anything."

"And ye've my eternal thanks." Teagan rested his hand over Greer's. "That couldnae have been easy."

According to her father, once he was finally able to escape the pirates, Greer's husband had died, and she was back at Randolph's. So he reevaluated how he wanted to go about things.

First, he returned to the village only to discover Cecille and Julianna had come and gone and were with the MacLauchlins. From there, he tracked everyone, waiting for the opportunity to strike. He knew Randolph would see him dead for taking the jewels, so he'd had a missive sent saying he had already died. That way, the lout would never see him coming when he struck.

"'Twas not easy deciding who to follow when they split off," Father said, referring to their pursuers. "Bartholomew or Randolph." He looked at Teagan. "In the end, I knew Cecille and Greer were safe with you and your warriors, so I continued after Randolph lest he reach Julianna before anyone else."

"'Twas a wise decision," Teagan replied. "I would have done the same." Amusement lit his eyes. "I give ye a great deal of credit, though. 'Tis no average man who can evade my brother Malcolm when he's tracking. For surely yer paths nearly crossed."

"Yes." The corner of her father's mouth shot up. "Let's just say your brother is very good, but I have a few years on him." He winked. "Plus, time spent with pirates teaches one a thing or two."

That it did, and her father spun many a tale about it as the night wore on.

"I see where ye get yer gift of storytelling," Teagan murmured in her ear at one point, dropping a chaste kiss on her cheek. She knew he wanted to do more, to kiss her lips and neck, to hold her close, but would see her respected in front of her parents.

Her parents, however, did no such thing. They kissed and held hands, barely taking their eyes off one another.

"How did I not see how affectionate they were?" she said later on when she and Teagan sat in their room, enjoying a last cup of ale. "How good a friendship they had? How in love they were?"

"Mayhap ye were too young to recognize it?" He shook his head. "Or mayhap, having known yer uncle, 'twas not something encouraged in 'proper' company."

"That would make sense." For none were less affectionate.

"I don't want that for us," she said softly, meaning it, keeping with the truth. "I want a life where we might be affectionate in the open as my parents were tonight." She shook her head. "I want our children to never wonder how we feel about one another. I want them to see…love as it should be."

She swallowed hard, fairly shocked she'd said love. But she meant it.

"I want the same, lass." He took her hand. "I want…love as it should be."

He felt it, too, didn't he? What had grown so quickly betwixt them? What would grow stronger still if they laid their hearts bare? If they unburdened their truths?

"'Tis time to talk, aye?" he said softly.

"Yes," she said just as softly. "'Tis time to talk."

Chapter Twenty-Seven

TEAGAN WAITED PATIENTLY as Greer gathered her thoughts. When she began to speak but stopped several times, then wrung her hands, he realized just how hard this was for her.

"'Tis all right, lass." He crouched in front of her and covered her trembling hands with his own. "Ye dinnae need to do this now. Ye've all the time in the world."

"No, I *do* need to do this now." She closed her eyes for a moment before she looked at him again. "'Tis just so hard to go back there…to see it all again."

"I ken." Going off the pain in her gaze, she'd been scarred deeply. "I ken because as ye saw this morn, I face difficult memories as well." He cupped her cheek. "But I will, with ye. We will do it together." He wrapped a blanket around her and then sat with her on his lap. "Why not start with why ye said ye knew me in those moments when I lost control on Bartholomew."

"I think I need to start a little further back than that," she whispered, swallowing hard before she found her voice again. "I should start at the beginning. The moment my friend and I decided to visit a village on the French border."

He frowned, not liking the sound of that.

"We were young and had no idea how dangerous it would be." Greer stared at the fire, someplace else. She shook her head. "In truth, though we'd heard rumor of how bad the war had become, we thought ourselves invincible." She pressed her lips together, struggling. "Our parents would have never allowed us to go there. They thought us visiting friends, but we were adventurous...and so very, very foolish."

His body grew more and more tense.

"Alfred was soldiering in the area at the time, so we thought ourselves all that much more invincible." A tear trickled down her cheek. "It really was such a lovely day. Sunny and warm." Her voice grew wobbly. "But then I suppose what kind of day it was matters naught."

"It *does* matter," he said softly, recalling all too well how much the little things mattered during wartime. Most especially when trying to grasp on to anything good. "I remember a day much like that. The temperature was just right, the sky cloudless and blue."

"As though nothing bad could happen beneath it," she went on. "We laughed so much, truly enjoying the villagers. The children, women, all of them. They were so welcoming." A soft smile curled her lips. "And it gave me a chance to practice my French."

"They were innocents," he whispered, there with her, understanding perfectly. "Yet so bloody vulnerable. Unprotected."

"Yes," she murmured. "So very unprotected." Her eyes remained glazed. A smile lingered. "I still remember my friend throwing back her head and laughing at something one of the children said." Greer's smile faded. "Then someone called out we were under attack."

"Aye," he continued on. "With but a single soldier to protect ye."

"Yes, Alfred...I..." Greer closed her eyes again as if trying not to see her past before she forced them open. Made herself see. Faced it. "Warriors were everywhere, cutting down men, women, and children as if they'd caused them some great affront. As though their lives had no meaning."

"Men turned monster," he whispered, seeing the carnage all over again. The broken bodies.

The soldier over the near-lifeless woman.

"We had no idea which way to go." Greer flexed her hand. "I tried to keep hold of my friend, but we got separated in the mayhem." Another tear rolled down her cheek. "Alfred managed to hide me and another woman in a cottage." She put a finger to her lips. "Quiet, he mouthed. Do not breathe a word."

Teagan brushed away her tear and waited for her to go on.

"Then he stood inside the door and waited with his blade in hand." More tears. "Would they open the door? Was that the end?" She touched her ear. "I could hear the cries of pain, the awful sounds of..." She inhaled a ragged breath. "You could not imagine the guilt I felt. The cowardice. I should have been out there doing anything I could to help..."

She trailed off and swallowed hard again before her gaze finally drifted to his face. "But I did not. I stayed there, trapped in terror. Useless. Helpless. Waiting for my certain death." She shook her head. "But they never came...they never opened the door." Though her eyes turned to the fire, he knew she peered into the past. "When it grew quiet enough, I crawled to the window, praying to God, hoping they weren't all dead. That my friend...my very best friend..."

He barely breathed, feeling not just his pain but hers. So very much of hers.

"The animal horn window had a crack I could peer through, but the lighting was so dim I could barely see." More silent tears. "But I saw *her*..." Greer's gaze drifted to his face again. "And I think I saw you defending her...then covering her, praying over her..." Her breathing grew choppier. "Holding her hand when she left..." She tried to speak again and couldn't. Eventually, she managed a few shaky words. "When Margery left...when she died."

"Och," he murmured, seeing it all so clearly now. Greer had been one of the lasses Alfred got out of there that day. "I cannae tell ye how sorry I am." He clenched his jaw, angry all over again. "Had I just gotten there sooner, mayhap..."

"Mayhap what?" she said softly. Her brows drew together. "What could you have done against so many?"

"I might have had time to get more men," he ground out. "At the verra least, I might have gotten to Margery before she was harmed. I could have stopped it before it ever happened."

"Perhaps." Greer shook her head. "Or perhaps not. It could be you were cut down first, and she died regardless." She threaded her fingers with his, in the moment again, rather than the past. "You were there when you were meant to be there, Teagan." Another tear trickled down her cheek. "There to salvage her dignity and lend her comfort in her final moments when I could not." Her voice cracked. "I could not even give her a proper burial or say goodbye."

"Ye did the only thing ye could, lass." He shook his head, heart-broken she'd had to see all that. "Had ye run out there, ye would have suffered the same fate." He squeezed her hand. "And Margery wouldnae have wanted that for ye."

"But perhaps if Alfred and I had faced things together, we could have—"

"Nay." He cupped her cheek, making sure her gaze stayed with him. "There were others about that day, Greer. Even as Margery was attacked. Too many for ye and Alfred to face alone. Yer cousin took the verra best course of action he could have. It ensured yer survival." He shook his head. "Understand that, lass. Understand that ye were where ye needed to be and 'twas not cowardice. Ye knew naught about fighting, and even if ye did, ye would have been outnumbered."

She managed a nod but gave no response.

"As to Margery having a proper burial, 'twas seen to." He brushed her tears away. "Edmund and I saw them all buried and prayed for."

"Thank God," she whispered, leaning her cheek into his touch. More tears fell. "Thank you… Thank you both so much. I never knew…"

"Ye dinnae need to thank us," he replied. "Margery was laid to rest in the end. Someday, if circumstances allow it, I will take ye to her burial site."

"I would like that." She rested her head against his shoulder. Silent tears kept falling. "Very much so."

"What happened to the other lass who was with ye?" he asked. "Did she survive?"

"Yes." She nodded. "Alfred got us both out safely."

"Good." He stroked her hair and stared at the fire as she worked through her grief and hopefully found some closure. Something he realized he found as well, knowing her and the other lass got away. That at least *they* survived that day.

"Margery will always be with ye, Greer," he eventually murmured, trying to offer her comfort. "She will always be in yer heart."

"And in my mind." She wiped away her tears, her gaze soft when she looked at him. "But I think you already know that."

"Aye." He brushed a lock of hair away from her eye. "I'm glad she's kept ye company over the years."

"You do not think me mad, then?"

"I think ye the furthest thing from it." He cupped the side of her delicate neck. "'Tis better she was with ye. That she gave ye strength, comfort, and mayhap even amusement when ye needed it."

"She did do that," she murmured. "I have a feeling I won't be hearing from her much anymore."

"Whether ye do or not, she's always welcome." He tilted her chin until their gazes aligned. "Ye ken, aye? She's always welcome with us MacLauchlins."

The corner of her mouth curved up. "That's kind of you to say."

"And verra much meant," he replied. "Whether she's real or not, she's part of ye, Greer. Part of everything that got ye to this moment."

Her brows swept up, and her lips curled higher. "Do you truly think her real?"

"One never knows." He grinned. "Or so Aunt Mórag would say."

"Ah, yes." Though still a tad wobbly, her smile grew. "She who should get along just fine with Ada."

"To be sure." He brushed away another tear, glad to see fewer falling now. "I look forward to ye meeting her. All of the MacLauchlins for that matter."

"Me, too." She yawned, her voice a faint murmur as she rested her head against his shoulder again. "But perhaps a bit of rest first."

He didn't blame her for being exhausted, considering the trauma of the day.

"Aye." He brought her to the bed. "Rest, indeed."

Or so he thought when he found her asleep before he even had the chance to lay her down.

Chapter Twenty-Eight

When lightning flashed, and thunder rumbled, Greer jolted awake, unsure where she was. When the lightning flashed again and illuminated Teagan's face, she realized she was tucked against his side, warm beneath the blankets.

She had no recollection of falling asleep or of him bringing her to bed.

Inhaling his scent, she curled her fingers against the heat of his broad chest and admired his masculine features. Admired the man he was all the way around. It was hard to believe how far they had come in so little time. How free she felt. Not just that, but fully present. *Here.* Not in a painful past or the in-between she'd existed in since, but right here.

What were the odds Teagan had been there that fateful day? That he was, in fact, the warrior-hero she'd built her fictional heroes around? The kindness and compassion he'd shown Margery had meant so very much to her. In its own way, his actions had given her cause to go on. To not give up on humanity altogether.

She rolled on her side and watched him slumber. Though tempted to touch him, to run her fingers along his strong jawline, she didn't want to wake him. For he, too, had faced much this eve. A past that haunted him. Moments that had stayed with him.

Yet it seemed he was awake, anyway, when he turned his head her way and opened his eyes. He didn't say anything but simply stared at her, his look so raw and loving her chest tightened.

It *was* love.

She had no idea how she knew, only that she did. It felt imprinted on her heart. Part of her soul.

She wanted more, though.

All of him.

She wanted to be his wife in every sense of the word.

Seeming to sense it, or simply wanting it himself, he propped himself up on an elbow, held her gaze a moment longer, then brushed his lips over hers. Once, twice, before he kissed her more deeply.

He tasted of man and ale as his tongue wrapped with hers, and his kisses grew hungry. Eager. All-consuming. As if he couldn't get enough of her. Heat flared beneath her skin when he cupped her cheek and kissed her deeper still. So deeply and so thoroughly, she grew desperate.

Impatient.

At some point, he'd gotten her out of her boots and dress, but she was still in her chemise. He, in turn, still wore his blasted breeches.

"Teagan," she groaned, aching for him. "Please."

The juncture between her legs throbbed and ached, making her all that much more impatient. Evidently understanding, or equally impatient, he rolled her beneath him, his kisses ravenous now. Fire consumed her as they tore at each other's clothes.

There was no slow build this time but a raging inferno of lust. Of hands and fingers, lips and tongues, of slick skin and heavy breathing. He yanked her chemise up, freed himself from his breeches, and settled between her thighs.

Thunder crashed, and rain pounded as his mouth found hers again, their kisses out of control. Urgent and frantic. Needful and desperate. She spread her legs wider and thrust her hips, eager for him to fill her, to assuage the brutal yet exquisite ache pulsing in her core.

"Och, lass," he whispered in a strangled voice, finally giving her what she needed.

He wrapped his fingers with hers by her head and pressed into her.

Rather than filling her with one quick thrust, he, bit by bit, gave her time to adjust to his girth. Their gazes held, the moment transcendent. As though they crossed some great divide and found each other on another plane. Her every nerve-ending came alive. Her sheer awareness of him making her his. Of being deeper and deeper inside her until he was fully seated.

She trembled with emotion, sensation, and awareness. With feelings she never thought possible. Love and desire. Lust and intoxicating pleasure. Teagan's shoulders and arms flexed with his barely constrained need. With how he fought to hold back and not frighten her. To be gentle when the raging desire between them made holding back a struggle.

"Please," she whimpered, pleading with her eyes. She gripped his back. Wrapped a leg around him.

Pushed to his brink, he released a strangled groan and moved, thrusting slowly at first, then harder. Deeper. Lost in the feel of it, *him*, she moaned with pleasure, marveling at how good this felt.

How good it could be.

Should be.

Gone in the moment, immersed in the way his body felt against her, *in* her, she wrapped her other leg around him. Taking her cue, just as eager, he moved faster, rolling his hips as he thrust. Driving her higher and higher.

Quaking with the force of it, the exquisite liquid-hot pleasure blossoming inside, she dug her nails into his back and met his thrusts. Again and again, over and over, until she hit a crescendo that knocked the wind right out of her.

One moment she chased pleasure, a cresting wave, the next, she rocketed right over the edge. His roar met her cry of release, and he pressed deep, filling her with his hot seed. She locked up, then shook all over, her body pulsing, near vibrating.

They stayed that way for a time, holding onto each other, immersed in the moment before he peppered kisses on her neck, jawline, then lips. Eventually, his gaze found hers again.

She wasn't sure what happened when their eyes locked during such an intimate moment, only that it felt like coming home. Like she'd found where she was supposed to be. Who she was supposed to be with.

"Is this love?" she whispered, swept up in more emotions than she could make sense of. Vaguely aware of a tear slipping down her cheek.

"Aye." He brushed his lips against hers. "I would say so."

He kissed her again and again, murmuring against her lips that he'd never felt this way before. That this had to be love. That she meant everything to him.

She lost track of how many murmured endearments he whispered in her ear as the night wore on, and they lost themselves in one another. Sometimes they made love slowly, other times more intensely. Sometimes so passionately she wept, other times so playfully she laughed.

By the time they drifted off, she knew what she felt was most certainly love. They stood at the threshold of a wonderful new life. Everything was going to be different now.

"Och, but look at ye," Ada mused when she gave Greer a hug hello the next morning. They had arrived around the time she and Teagan finally found their way downstairs. Her friend's knowing gaze went from Teagan to Greer. "Ye're a whole new lass, ye are."

"I am." She smiled at Teagan because she couldn't help herself. "A whole new lass, to be sure."

"We missed ye, Mistress Greer." Besse flung her arms around Greer's waist. "Though 'twas great fun with Edmund the Defender."

"Ye mean Edmund the Protector," Duncan corrected, embracing her as well. "For he snuck us away from the evil sorcerer."

"Then defended us," Greer pointed out.

"More like Edmund the Scoundrel," Ada muttered under her breath. There was no missing the pinkening of her cheeks when she eyed the Englishman, though. Nor the small smile she shot his way when she thought no one was looking.

Rather than linger at the tavern, introductions were made, and everyone set out straight away.

"'Tis a beautiful day for riding," Teagan whispered in her ear. "A beautiful day to take ye home."

It was, too.

In fact, it was as beautiful out as that fretful day years ago.

"And 'twill stay beautiful this time," Margery would say. "'Twill stay beautiful always."

The sky did stay blue. To top it all off, a vibrant colored sunset blazed on the horizon when they finally crested the hill, and she saw MacLauchlin Castle for the first time. Though Teagan had spoken at length about it, his words didn't do it justice.

Cozied between verdant pines with a sparkling ocean backdrop, it felt like home.

She looked over her shoulder at him. "'Tis truly lovely, husband."

"Aye." His gaze lingered on her face. "As are ye, wife."

By the time they made it over the drawbridge and into the courtyard, a host of people waited, but she only had eyes for one.

"Dear God, is that her?" she murmured, taking in the beautiful young girl looking from her to her parents. Greer blinked back tears. "Is that Julianna?"

The last time she'd seen her, she was a little girl, crying that she didn't want to leave her sister and father. As soon as Teagan helped her down, she headed Julianna's way, only for her sister to meet her halfway in an embrace.

"How I missed you, little sister." She held on tight, cupping the back of Julianna's head. "More than you can possibly imagine."

"I missed you, too," Julianna replied, sniffling.

Moments later, their parents wrapped their arms around them, as well, and held on just as tight. In all the wild tales she'd spun to keep going over the years, she had never imagined coming together with her family again like this. Holding them in her arms, knowing they were safe.

"I'm so glad you all returned safely," Julianna said when the embrace ended. She wiped away tears and looked at their father. "I thought you were dead." She sniffled some more. "I thought…"

"No, dear daughter." Father embraced her again. "Not dead but very much alive."

"A story we are eager to hear," Keenan said, introducing himself and his wife, Fionna.

A story, as it happened, that commenced with an even happier ending than any foresaw.

Chapter Twenty-Nine

"'Tis truly a gracious offer," Keenan said later that evening as everyone enjoyed a dram of whisky in front of the fire. He shook Phillip's hand. "'Tis more than expected."

"'Tis the least I can do for a clan who has done so very much for my family." His sentimental gaze went to his wife and daughters. "If not for you MacLauchlins, I dread to think where they would be now." He nodded at Keenan, Malcolm, and Teagan. "You have my undying gratitude."

They nodded in return, and Keenan raised a mug in toast. "Here's to new friends and alliances."

Phillip raised his as well. "Indeed!"

Everyone raised theirs in turn, celebrating a bright new beginning. How could they not when Phillip was giving the MacLauchlins not just Greer's substantial dowry, but an alliance with a noble English family and, most of all, the gem that tied them to King Edward III himself. It put them in a unique position and, if need be, would see their clan protected.

While Phillip made it clear they could use the gem for whatever they liked, Teagan knew Keenan would hold on to it for him. That it was, in its way, a means to protect Greer if anything went awry. As it were, her dowry alone brought substantial wealth to their clan.

Wealth that he would trade in a heartbeat to keep her in his arms and safe. Protected and cherished. Free to think and say what she would.

"How did yer conversation with Isabella go?" he murmured in Greer's ear, glad to have her on his lap, in his arms. "Is she all right?"

Greer had sat down with Isabella earlier and spoken of her sister's passing when she caught an illness a few years back. How peaceful it had been in the end. How much she loved Isabella.

"She's all right," Greer confirmed. "Though 'twas hard, I think it gave her closure."

"Aye." He squeezed her hand. "No doubt it did."

While mayhap a bit subdued, Isabella seemed at peace on Malcolm's lap, her hand resting over his on her swollen belly. He nuzzled her neck often, his love for her so recognizable to Teagan now, he couldn't imagine how he'd ever wondered at it. His gaze went to Keenan and Fionna, who barely took their eyes off each other, then to Greer's parents, who did the same.

Love was all around him.

Right next to him.

He brushed his lips across Greer's temple, remembering the eve before. How sweet it had been making love to her. How much he longed to do it time and time again until her belly swelled. Then plenty more as the years went on.

"*Très bien alors les petits,*" Fulbert exclaimed, shooing Duncan and Besse along. He had come here with Isabella from France and loved cooking almost as much as her. "All right, little ones, let's go get what we made." He cocked a brow at Julianna and Dougal in passing. "Come along then. You are never too old for this."

Greer eyed Keenan and Fionna's son and Julianna as they followed. "Is it me, or are they walking a tad bit close?"

"Shh, dinnae get yer mother started." He chuckled. "She's convinced love blossoms betwixt the two and considers Julianna too young."

"I imagine she does," Greer replied softly. "Though, in truth, she's almost marrying age."

"Aye," he agreed. "But trust me, ye'd do well not to say such in front of yer good ma."

"Point taken." Her gaze drifted to Ada and Edmund, who had danced a turn or two earlier but sat apart now, eyeing one another. "I would say young love is not all that blossoms."

"Nay." He chuckled. "They eye one another like predator and prey, do they not?"

"They do." She met his chuckle. "Yet one has to wonder, who is the prey and who the predator?"

"'Tis, without doubt, a game of cat and mouse."

She grinned at him. "You mean cats and dogs."

He met her grin. "We are never going to let them forget that, are we?"

Her brows arched. "Now, what fun would there be in that?"

"None at all."

He was about to say more when Fulbert and the young ones returned with pastries to celebrate not just Teagan and Greer's matrimony but a bright new future for the MacLauchlins.

"I will miss them when they are gone," Greer murmured. She enjoyed the delicacy and watched her parents. "I wish they could stay on longer."

Her parents would be staying a few days, then heading back to England while Julianna stayed on for now.

"They willnae be gone permanently, lass," he reminded. "They need to get things established at yer estate and groom Alfred to take over. Until then, 'tis important they oversee things and make what they expect clear."

"I know," she said softly. "I will still miss them, though."

"Aye, but ye will have all of us to keep ye company until their return." He smiled and dusted frosting off her nose, chuckling as Aunt Mórag call out to Ada that it was time. "And 'tis bound to be verra entertaining around here."

"Aye, I'm coming," Ada called back, finishing off her pastry. She told her children to keep an eye on Edmund the Scoundrel, and to be good, then she was off.

"Better hurry up," Mórag muttered. "The spirits willnae wait all moonrise."

"What is it they are doing again?" Greer shook her head as Edmund admired Ada's backside. "Walking to the ocean?"

"Aye." Teagan smiled softly as his aunt and Ada vanished outside. "It seems with ours being the final marriage that brings good fortune to the MacLauchlins, Aunt Mórag's ready to go to the sea. There she will wish the husband and son she lost to the illness a safe journey into the afterlife."

"That's nice," Greer murmured. "And Ada will help her do that?"

"So, she says." He nodded at Colmac and Rona across the way. "Either way, it does all of us, especially her eldest son and daughter-in-law, good to see her out and about again. Free from the binds that held her."

"I get that." Greer polished off her pastry and leaned back against him. "So very much."

"Aye." He rested his cheek against her temple, knowing she'd faced her demons every bit as much as he had his. "For we are free now, too, are we not?"

"We are," she whispered. "So very free."

While they would always carry a bit of their past with them, it was no longer all-consuming. No longer took them away from the here and now.

"And what of your good friend Edmund?" Greer winked. "Or should I say, half-brother?" He had one of Ada's bairns on each knee, all three of them covered in pastry droppings. "Do you think his grand adventure will end here?"

"Nay, I think 'twill *begin* here." He smiled and toasted Edmund when he looked his way. "I think yer wee Scottish friend already has him cast beneath her spell."

"You realize that could very well be a *real* spell?"

"Aye, but then I guarantee 'twould be just the sort of way my brother-in-arms would want to fall in love," he responded. "Like I said, the perfect beginning to his grand new adventure."

She was about to respond when a commotion came at the door.

"Och, 'tis good to be home!" his sister Nessa declared, entering with her new husband, Tavish. "Hello, brothers!"

Unbeknownst to all, Nessa and Fionna's first-in-command had been carrying on a secret affair for years. One that finally came to light when Fionna and Keenan came together, their clans no longer enemies.

Though Nessa had been home a few times since she and Tavish married, she spent more time at the Taylor holding. Introductions were made, and as expected, the celebration resumed as the MacLauchlin clan finally came back together. The pipes sprang to life, and dancing began anew.

Teagan couldn't remember the last time he laughed so much nor spent so much time in the present. But he did and always would with Greer.

Eventually, he pulled her close, eager to be alone with her again. "Are ye ready to—"

"I thought you would never ask," she replied before he could finish. Her cheeks were flushed, and her eyes dewy with desire. "Yes, husband, I am *very* much ready to."

So they did, day after day, only falling more deeply in love if that were possible.

Though he had fulfilled his pact with his brothers, in the end, he'd found so much more than he could have hoped for. Not just the wealth his clan needed, but the cure to his broken heart. Greer had saved him from the dark corners of his mind, the brutality of mankind, and his own guilty conscience.

More than that, she had shown him the light again.

She had, in every sense of the word, been his redemption and the start to a wonderful new life.

Epilogue

A year and a half later…

"'Tis hard to believe we stood here two years ago today, and I asked ye to make such a pact." Keenan shook his head at his brothers. "It seems almost callous now, aye?"

They stood in the woodland just beyond the castle.

"'Twas the best bloody thing ye ever did." Malcolm clasped his brothers' shoulders. "I cannae imagine where we would be if ye hadnae."

"'Tis not worth imagining." Teagan shook his head and nodded at Keenan. "Ye saved our lives with that pact, brother."

"Bloody hell right, he did." Fionna grinned as she joined them. "Rumor had it ye three might be out here getting all sentimental." She pulled skins out of a satchel. "So, I brought some whisky to celebrate the amazing lasses that came into yer lives."

"And I brought you some bannock *fraîchement sorti du four*, fresh out of the oven," Isabella said, setting down a basket of bread.

"And I am but a reminder of just how important that pact was," Greer said softly, joining them with their newborn little girl, with her shock of black hair. She smiled at Teagan. "Our wee one did not want to miss the celebration."

"Nor should she." He kissed his daughter's forehead. "'Tis her celebration as well, after all."

Where he thought Greer was the epitome of all things good, he realized God could bring him even more goodness with his daughter. With something so precious, there was no longer room for his demons. No longer room for his past. Only his future.

Where Fionna and Keenan had merged their households, Fionna was still as much in charge as his brother, standing side by side with him in all things. Isabella had since joined ranks with the head cook and regularly served fare that kept them all very happy. As he knew would be the case, Malcolm's eyes never strayed, the deep love he and his wife shared the envy of many a young romantic.

As to Greer, she and Fulbert had seen a new chapel built so that their people might have somewhere to worship and keep the faith. When not busy seeing to that, one could often find her by Ada and Mórag's side, in front of a fire spinning tales for the wee bairns.

Between their renewed affiliation with the Campbells and Isabella and Greer's dowries, they'd been able to truly begin rebuilding their clan. Thick tapestries now lined the castle walls, and though rushes still lay by the front door, carpets adorned the floors everywhere else. Furnishings were made, and crop seeds sewn. More defenses were built and cottages added. Their stables were filling with horses and their armory with new blades.

"Hold your positions," Edmund declared, as though leading a charge. "We are almost there!" He stomped through the forest with a bunch of children. Malcolm's son was on his left shoulder and Keenan's daughter on his right. Ada's Duncan led the charge with a wooden sword and her Besse, a wooden dagger.

"Och, ye've still a long way to go, Sassenach," Ada countered. She cooed at her and Edmund's wee son swaddled in her arms with his shock of red hair. "But ye're getting closer."

"Bloody hell right, we are, wife." He winked at Dougal and Julianna, who pulled their hands apart when they realized Cecille followed. "'Tis just a matter of keeping an eye to our surroundings when the enemy approaches."

"Language," Dougal warned, winking at Edmund in return. "For ye are always being watched."

"That's right." Ada gave Edmund a look, then a small smile just for him. "*And* heard."

"Indeed," Cecille agreed as she and Phillip joined them. She narrowed her eyes at Julianna and Dougal before she smiled at Teagan and his brothers. "We heard there might be a celebration out this way."

Keenan shook his head and eyed his brothers. "Ye talk too much."

Fionna nudged him. "As do ye, husband."

"I think ye all do," Aunt Mórag said, joining them as well. She'd come out of her seclusion entirely now and apprenticed other healers. No longer the haughty, self-important aunt from their childhood, she was now known as the healing witch of their clan. Accepted for her odd ways, even by the God-fearing folk.

Keenan eyed the lot of them. "Is that everyone then?"

"Almost," Nessa called out. She and Tavish headed their way with their wee lassie, who insisted on toddling along rather than being carried. "We've a stubborn daughter, we do."

"As do we a stubborn son," Rona called out from behind them as she and Colmac's son toddled right after his cousin.

"Almost there," Colmac assured them, grinning at his boy the whole way.

"Well, then," Keenan finally said. He shook his head with amusement at the bairns trying to over-talk each other as he made his toast to his brothers and their much-increased family. He raised his skin and smiled, looking from Fionna and their children to his brothers. "Here's to getting far more than we bargained for when we made our pact."

"Aye." Malcolm pulled Isabella close and rested his hand on her slightly swollen stomach. "Everything we never knew we needed."

"Without a doubt." Teagan pulled Greer and their wee one close as well. "The verra best life has to offer."

"Here's to that!" Aunt Mórag agreed.

They all raised their skins and toasted a pact that changed life as they knew it. That wiped away the years of suffering, illness, and warfare, letting each and every one of them move on.

To find love.

Happiness.

A much-needed start to a happy new life.

In the end, their Highlander's pact wasn't one made by scoundrels, but by the men they were supposed to be. The past they were meant to leave behind. The future they were destined to embrace. Most importantly, though, the women and children that made it all possible, giving them far more than wealth ever could.

About the Author

Sky Purington is the bestselling author of over fifty novels and novellas. A New Englander born and bred who recently moved to Virginia, Purington married her hero, has an amazing son who inspires her daily and two ultra-lovable husky shepherd mixes. Passionate for variety, Sky's vivid imagination spans several romance genres, including historical, time travel, paranormal, and fantasy. Expect steamy stories teeming with protective alpha heroes and strong-minded heroines.

Purington loves to hear from readers and can be contacted at Sky@SkyPurington.com. Interested in keeping up with Sky's latest news and releases? Either visit Sky's website, www.SkyPurington.com, join her quarterly newsletter, or sign up for personalized text message alerts. Simply text 'skypurington' (no quotes, one word, all lowercase) to 74121 or visit Sky's Sign-up Page. Texts will ONLY be sent when there is a new book release. Readers can easily opt out at any time.

Love social networking? Find Sky on Facebook, Instagram, Twitter, and Goodreads.

Want a few more options? "Follow" Sky Purington on Amazon to receive New Release Kindle Updates and "Follow" Sky on BookBub to be notified of amazing upcoming deals.